T0166819

THE MYSTIC MASSEUR'S WIFE

Publisher's note

It proved impossible to represent some of the names and words deriving from Hindi and Bhojpuri in the way the author wished. This concerned the use of an 'a' with a macron to represent a 'long' 'a' in a number words such as: achār, ālu, Ārya Samaj, Ātmā, bachā, bachiyā, bhav sāgar, Bābā, Bābu, Bāp, Bhāgavid Gita, Bhāgvat, Bhagwān, Brāhman, Chāchi, Dādā, Dādi, Gangā, jamāt, Kākā, Kāki, kanyādān, kathā, kutyā, lāwa, lorhā, Mahā Sabhā, Māmi, Māmu, Mātā, Narayān, panditāye, Poophā, Purānas, Rādhayshyam, Rāja, Rāmāyan, Rāmdass, Rāmlogan, Rāmsumair, sādhu, sārhi, sāri, Shāstri, singhāsan, Sitarām, sohārie, tāssa, Vyāsa, wāli. The above representation was achieved graphically, a method too unreliable and time-consuming to be practical throughout the novel.

The quotations from that earlier version of the lives of Ganesh and Leela Ramsumair on page 99 and 106 come, of course, from V.S. Naipaul's novel, *The Mystic Masseur* (1957).

Printed in the United Kingdom by Severn, Gloucester,
on responsibly sourced paper.

J. VIJAY MAHARAJ

THE MYSTIC MASSEUR'S WIFE

PEEPAL TREE

First published in Great Britain in 2022
Peepal Tree Press Ltd
17 King's Avenue
Leeds LS6 1QS
England

© 2022 J. Vijay Maharaj

ISBN13: 9781845235338

Supported using public funding by
ARTS COUNCIL
ENGLAND

CONTENTS

Put it at its simplest: was I funny, or was I serious? So many tones of voice were possible or assumable, so many attitudes to the same material.
— V.S. Naipaul, *The Enigma of Arrival*

I recognise the place, I feel at home here, but I don't belong. I am of, and not of, this place.

— V.S. Naipaul, *A New World Order*

ALMOST A PROLOGUE TO A SONG

Forty years ago, I listened to Leela Ramsumair tell the story of her life and discovered another version of the tombstone riddles that proliferate in these parts: "She was a mother without knowing it and a wife without letting her husband know it except by her kind indulgences to him." But, of course, like any other story worth telling, hers also had features unique to her. I must touch on some of these briefly in this prologue to her story.

In telling her own story, Mrs Ramsumair narrated those of others, interestingly more often about her husband's family rather than her own lineage. This may be so since I went looking for her because we all knew something about the husband. But I think, too, that although she was to an extent modern, given that she was born in 1911 and lived through one of the most fertile periods of modernisation in the Caribbean, in the way of 'ancient' women she seemed to consider herself as belonging to her husband's lineage. She spoke of her father-in-law, Baba, with great love, and recalled many of his stories including what he told her about how and why his own father, whom he called Babu, came from India as a child with his father and mother and about how his mother, Mai, died on the voyage. Apparently Babu's father had some of the usual reasons for taking his little family on the road into indentureship, but the rest is more or less the familiar indenture story of hardships endured followed by triumph.

Her focus on her in-laws could also stem from the fact that she knew much more about that family because of her closeness to Baba who spoke about these things, than she did of her own family because her father didn't. In retrospect, her family's story seemed to begin and end with the nucleus of her father, mother and sister embedded in the village of Four Ways in which Baba was a central figure. Indeed, she gives us a very good sense of this place and community from which her husband Ganesh came. I myself came to know Four Ways as a community teeming with life and activity, from which Ganesh is banished in more ways than one, but to which Leela managed to return. In this way, she also revealed many little-known aspects of her husband's story that are interesting for those who knew or have heard of him. The many stories she told bobbed and weaved in my imagination as she spoke them aloud in cadences of a lovely song, and I discovered that they had lost none of these qualities when I returned to them.

The rediscovery occurred while I was recently doing something similar to what the Scandinavians and others call döstädning. There were the tapes I had made while she spoke. And there were the folders of her songs and newspaper clippings that she had also carelessly told me to take because she said she no longer needed such encumbrances. As I listened to them, I not only enjoyed the stories again, but I also realised my own amateurishness especially in the absence of probing questions that come to mind now that didn't then. Nonetheless the urgency of transcribing what she said became a clear and mandatory part of my own housecleaning process. It wasn't a difficult job. Indeed, it was one that I enjoyed and in which I became the more engrossed the further along I went. Despite my shortcomings as an amateur, maybe your experience will be similar and I want to take the opportunity now to wish you happy reading.

CHAPTER 1: FATAL DAYS

It does always have a best place to start a story, eh? And to tell you the truth, much a what you asking me for, how you say? – Leela Ramsumair story – really start, happen and end in the absence a Ganesh Ramsumair and the consequences a he absence, although I still kinda have to tell you he own to tell you mine. One a the most important event was death, and the death what connect the pieces a my story together is my father-in-law one, although he wasn't my father-in-law when death did come for him. Because is that moment when Baba dead that bringing up everything you asking me about to the surface.

You see that was when – how you call it – the "adventurous life of this Indian woman in 1940s Trinidad", what you say I end up living, start up for true. Although, I have to tell you, if I think about it at all, I woulda think a myself as a Trinidadian woman. How the song go? "*A chic-a-chic boom chic boom / It's the Trinidad lady!*" I should also tell you that I never ever think a myself as adventurous. I think my life is and was about the fact that I does always do what I think is best for the people I care about, my family, a few friends who come like family and anybody else I could do something for – except for one little little time that mightn't even be a part a the story that you come looking for, when some things happen, like a shower a blessings from above, just for me and me alone.

To tell you the story properly, I should really really start after Pandit Ramsumair stop coming in the shop for he self because he say he can't catch he breath by the time he reach back home. So then I start walking up the hill with one or two things for him from Pa shop, mostly what I used to see him picking up for heself from time to time. Pa used to say, "Yes, yes. Go on. Carry it. Carry it. It good to keep a eye on what happening to him." I used to take the things to him as though I obedient to Pa, but I really going because I want to be with Pandit Ramsumair, not just to know if he alright, but to spend time with him, the same way I was doing ever since we did come to live in Ramsumair Piece.

Sometimes I used to carry some butter, sometimes I carry a few hops bread or biscuit with it or some alu, some oil, some Milo – whatever I find running a little low in the kitchen or what I remember he like, even though Shairoon Chachi, who used to clean and cook for him, used to always make sure everything in the house was top-a-the-line. I like to visit him so much because I remember good good, as if it happen just yesterday, how much he used to love to talk and how much books he did spend he days reading, what he did like to talk about, and how much I like to listen.

Ganesh move most a them books outta the house when we was going Fuente Grove and I can't remember now where we lost some a them along the way, but they used to be line-up on the wall right here behind my back on them bookshelf, just like how I does keep these books here up to now. And when I come by him, Baba used to read out to me from them sometimes, especially if I meet up with him in the middle a he reading. Like everybody else in this village, I used to call him Panditji sometimes and Baba mosta the time. He used to call me Bayté most a the time, or Bayt, or Bayti sometimes, and Radhayshyam sometimes too, just like he call all the other younger people in the village.

The only time he didn't call me any a them names was when I used to bring a tin a Canadian salmon for him. Them time, if he let me cook it for him, and we sitting down together after to eat, he might start up with something like, "Compa", or "Comrade", or, or sometimes "Dost", or sometimes "hum safar" or something to show how eating salmon putting him in a different kinda mood. He used to carry on like a real pandit on singhasan them time and say things like, "The Canadians banking we money and I banking some of they fish to keep me healthy and strong." It was some kinda joke and I always used to laugh. If he happy, I used to feel happy too.

Sometimes he used to remind me, he "hum safar", that the

Canadian bank and the Canadian missionaries them come here after we start coming from India with their eye train to save we from hell. And he say, "All a them continue to say the same thing from then to now, and up to now we don't really siddown and talk enough about whether they bringing or trying to take away, and what we should do about it either way."

That is the kinda thinking what make Baba take care Ganesh get schooling. He did want Ganesh to make he future different from what other people did describing for we. Most a the people in Four Ways was so. My father and all was the same. He and Ma send me and my sister, Soomintra Didi, to school too. We went to the CM school right here in Four Ways. To tell you the truth, I eh sure up to now if it did matter what kinda school you did go to, nah, because all a we used to have to read the same Captain J. O. Cutteridge *West Indian Readers* and *West Indian Arithmetic* and Captain Daniel *West Indian History*.

Baba went to the CM school so he know, but he must be had he own reasons for wanting he son to go to government school, and he fight up he best to make that happen. Schooling wasn't compulsory and free for everybody, you know, until 1961, just before independence. So, if you ask me, that was real forward thinking and behaviour on Baba part. I feel like Ganesh inherit plenty a Baba ways because he did have that same kinda forward thinking. Maybe even a little too much in some ways.

Is funny though eh, that even though Baba used to make that kinda joke, he continue to bank with the Canadians just like other people from all over, not only here but in other place like Jamaica, Cuba and Puerto Rico. And hear nah, them here since the nineteenth century and although people like we couldn't a bank there then, I still banking there up to today. I mean is only just the other day, after the black power revolution, that things start to change a little little bit in the bank and them.

Yes, you right. I suppose just like with independence, we will only stop dealing with them if and when *them* tell *we* that we not together no more. And I don't have to remind you that although Baba choose government school, we does still always hold the CM people in high regard. But that might be because we does hold everybody in high regard, RC, EC, CM, Baptist, Muslim,

11

Born Again – although maybe not so much as we own. Is just who we is I suppose. Baba even respect Henry C. McLeod, who was a bank manager.

I feel up to now, eh, that I was very very fortunate to make them trip up to this house I still think about as Baba house. I was lucky that I get a chance to be with him like that in them last days a he life – almost every day, you know – for two whole years. But long before that, it was finding Baba that make life a little better for me when Ma wasn't here no more. From the day I meet him for the first time, I start to feel like things going to be alright after Pa did move here and open back that shop after Ma and shopkeeper Dookhie dead.

According to Pa, Dookhie just dead, oui. Nobody don't know how. When Jordan son, Keston, went in the shop in the morning like he used to do every working morning a the year, it wasn't open and he went back home and tell he father. Jordan come to see for he self, dragging Keston behind him so he could buss some licks on him if he lying. When he see is true and he see that the doors lock from inside, he try all how to wake up Dookhie from outside. When nothing happen, he call them other fellas who was going to work that hour and they break down the door. They find Dookhie dead in he bed.

But Ma did dead from snakebite in the canefield in broad daylight with plenty people all around she. And when it happen Pa cuss way foreman Mycoo arse for making the woman them pick up trash for loading on the cart to carry to put round the fig plant and them in he fig patch by he house. Everybody used to say that that is where Mycoo used to hide the things he thief from the estate. He did want to make sure it always have thrash on top so nobody wouldn't suspect it there, but he did also want to make sure that he could still get them back quick quick whenever he want them. All a we did know what he used to do, but we didn't count.

Pa say afterwards that what Mycoo used to do wasn't bad compared to what some other foreman and overseer do. He remember the days when foreman used to be on your back when you to have to gather up the megasse or bagasse to feed the fire in the factory and that was hard and dangerous work because centipede, scorpion and snake does like to live in the heapa thrash people have to load up in the cart to carry to the factory. And is another story for the people who used to have to stoke the fire. But that time when Ma get bite, Pa say he wasn't thinking about nothing like that. Pa get fire on the spot for how he get on and he woulda get beat up bad too, maybe they might a even kill him, if he didn't pull out the gun from the back a he waist and fire one in the air, same time telling Mycoo badjohns to come closer so he could test to see if he bullet really doh like ugly, like Balo say when he was buying the gun from he.

In case you thinking something schupid like, "Oh what a horrible thing indentureship was!" I better tell you that nobody wasn't indenture on the estate anymore that time, but nothing didn't change from the years before, when it still had some who free paper didn't sign yet. As a matter a fact, everybody does say that the last three years was the worse and it get even more worse after, especially for the people who come in the last ship. But worse or worserer, it had some people who try their best to look out for one another and Panditji come to see we father to offer him a place to live that same night Ma dead, although nobody didn't know what he intention was because he just come to the wake like everybody else.

He come with a plan for how Pa could make a living from then on. Dookhie did dead just about a month before that and Dookhie didn't have no family. Was he one used to be there taking care a the shop and when Ma dead, Baba didn't have time to put nobody to run the shop after Dookhie dead. Baba tell Pa that he feel that he would do a good job as shopkeeper, maybe even a better job than Dookhie, seeing as how he wasn't fraid to stand up for he self.

You see, the shop was really Baba own because it on the bottom corner a he nine-acre piece. But he never interfere with what going on in the shop and he didn't charge no rent or nothing. Baba say that that is how things was since he father days. Same way Ganesh behave afterwards when he give the Maha Sabha a acre on the other side from the shop to build one a the school that them, and other groups, did start building fast fast once they get the chance. You must be know some a them. Arya Samaj? Anjuman

Sunnat-ul-Jamat Association? You must be hear about them schools too, ent? They used to call them coolie cowshed school but I don't know if they does call them that still. It was after the school build that Sonachan, the new shopkeeper after Pa retire, give up the spirituous license and turn the shop into a straight parlour for the children that you does still see spending every recess there up to today.

Sonachan and he wife and children get the house and the parlour when Pa come to live with we in town and them have it still. After I did come back here to live, one a Sonachan big son come and tell me, "Tanty, we go have to siddown and talk about deed and thing for the property whenever you have time nah." And I suppose the boy was right. Is not like longtime and the boy must be thinking that today, tomorrow, I close my eye and anything could happen to them. And, come to think of it, to this whole property that take up so much a Ganesh energy and effort in all we young days. When the boy tell me that, I tell him I go try to see if I can't get Ganesh advice about it, but even if I can't, I go talk to we lawyer, Kapildev. I was thinking that I might have to put the business a inheritance in order for myself nah. But – haha – like I forgetting. That is not what we talking about today.

We talking about when Baba talk to Pa. As soon as Baba done put the plan to him, Pa move outta the barracks quick sharp. Me and Soomintra Didi was only eight years and twelve years old that time. And we was crying and confused, but as soon as the funeral done, Pa one with he two little daughters move to the shop. So that is how come we grow up on that spot down the hill there right here on Ramsumair Piece. That is where Pa do head shaving and bhandara and everything for Ma, and Pa call Dookhie name too, because Dookhie didn't have nobody to do nothing for he.

Ramsumair Piece is how everybody used to call all these lands that Panditji father, Babu, and he two brothers what did come from India as children with their father, buy in parts after they decide that the best thing for them to do is stay in Trinidad. Was only about a hundred acres in all, not like them big big estate like Coeur de Jardin where Pa had it out with Mycoo, and a good bit a even the hundred acres did get take over for oil drilling. You know, is only when I get big, I know that the real name for this place where we living is Four Ways but I think it will always remain just Ramsumair Piece in my head.

That is why I call this centre what I put up here after I move back from town, the Ramsumair Institute for Cultural Peace. I take the motto for it from Dietrich Bonhoeffer who born the same year as Ganesh, in 1906, but he dead in 1945, long before Ganesh went England. Bonhoeffer was like plenty a we own calypsonians because he was a very strong opponent to Hitler and the Nazi dictatorship and wasn't fraid to say so. They hang him you know, poor fella, just before freedom from Hitler come and they say the war over.

The motto for the institute what I take from him is "Silence in the face of evil is itself evil: God will not hold us guiltless. Not to speak is to speak. Not to act is to act." None of we own calypsonians didn't say nothing like that and that is how come I use Bonhoeffer words. And is because I didn't want to keep silence about what some people was saying and doing that I did open the Institute in the first place. In a way, when I start up, I was probably trying to continue some a the work what Ganesh used to do before he turn he back just so, just so, and leave.

But back to Pa now. It was like Pa coulda never forget that day when Ma dead and how he try and try and try to suck out the poison from Ma foot with no success – suck and spit, suck and spit until they reach the hospital and the nurse tell him she done dead and what the hell wrong with he, if he trying to kill he self too. He can't forget all the trouble that land up on he head on that fatal day. I was only eight years old when all a this happen and most a what I know I didn't see with my own eye, you hear. But Pa tell we about it so much time that I feel like I see everything correct correct as it happen.

I does feel up to now, eh, like I could see the coral snake, three feet long and pretty like a necklace a jumbie beads, sliding away from Ma foot after it make the two puncture mark that Pa see when Doolarie Mausi start to bawl for help and Pa run go knowing that the trouble everybody waiting on patiently did finally come for he and the rest a we. Thank God, Baba reach out he hand to we and the trouble couldn't mash we up for good, like trouble mash up plenty other people in the canefield.

Even though we used to call him Panditji and he did have this same small kutya in the yard what I clean up and put back in order and does see about up to now, just like I used to see about it before I get marrid to Ganesh and went away, Pandit Ramsumair never do panditaye for nobody. I does always wonder about that. I really don't know why that was. Maybe it had something to do with the stories Baba tell we what he hear from Babu about he own father experience in India, about how the pandits couldn't make a living and how people did start to treat them like servants for the whole village. Whatever the reason, Baba and he brothers live just like the rest a we, although some a we strike out lucky and plenty people envy we for that, mostly because they don't know the whole story.

Is not no joke when they say that the biggest problem in this country is that people does live like crab in a barrel. But a person luck is a person luck and no dog or cat shouldn't envy nobody for what is their luck. But is so it is. And, you know, was pure luck that put some money in Baba and he brothers' hands. They was just three brothers, just like Babu and he two brothers what did come from India as boys with their father, but Baba and he brothers was luckier because they had a sister too. Babu and them was real unlucky. Their mother did dead on the boat while they was coming self and Baba grandfather did have to do a make-up funeral for he poor dulahin, a thing a man shoulda never have to do, and then he had to throw she in the water before the body could get purified in fire, which is the correct order a things. You could imagine how that man and he three sons must be feel? I don't think nobody could ever imagine.

Baba and he brothers and sister and their cousins finally get a little luck when they find oil in their land, although he heself never live long enough to enjoy it and after that, well everything turn old mas. In them days, when it happen, when the luck come to you, if your property had mineral or spring or pond on it, that was your one, your own personal property. But things didn't last long like that at all. Nobody not really comfortable with poor people getting rich and that is one a the truest truth on this island.

In we case is because this island, what Ganesh used to say does just pretend to be a island, is one a the place where petroleum born. So much people did start to make oil claims when they start drilling for oil down here in south eh, that they had was to pass new laws for selling land. The new law did mean that they start to give people deed to the surface but no rights to nothing that underneath.

These days, when people suffering for water, I does think about that sometimes. Because even if they have spring on their land, they can't use it for their own purpose because the water and all belong to the government. I feel that is why we don't know how to identify spring and how to find and mind the veins for the water to come to the surface anymore. The knowledge disappear and the water remaining under the ground and we have to rely on the old ones from before that time. Thank God government build well on top a some a them and run pipe from them. These things start happening after the Americans take over at Brighton, Baba used to say, and he insist that is Walter Darwent who put it in motion in 1866 and that black gold is really what Darwent and the Canadians follow and reach here.

You know, one time, when we did just just married, Ganesh tell me how he was damned vex with Baba because a how when he done reach fifteen years old and long past the age when real Brahman boys woulda get janeo, Baba and he big brother, who Ganesh and all a we used to call Dada, because that is how you does call your father big brother, shame him by bringing him back from Port of Spain to perform janeo on he. "Is the little money they get for the oil rights that went to their head," Ganesh say. And he did say how they did want everything they could get with it one time, and how they pick him to make all their dreams come true because Dada didn't have no children. They did want to make him Brahman and doctor or lawyer same time. He tell me that Dookhie, who he call a arsehole, tell him this is not India, this is Trinidad, when he try to walk away from the whole damned confusion. He say he feel he have to follow he real inheritance, the gift of listening to people and rubbing them and fixing their bones and pains, and reading and learning more every day to do he work better.

He say how the two of them – he was talking about Baba and Dada – think they was better than Kaka. This was a time when every manjack think they getting rich from oil. He tell me, "I hear Kaka bribe the scouts to drill all about inside he ten-acre piece and then take the money they offer and make it to St Joseph Road in Laventille where he settle down with he wife and family. And perhaps they was right, eh, because the drilling make almost all the rest a Kaka land worthless. I bet you the last time Kaka wear dhoti, kurta and topi and walk about looking schupid with a big black umbrella on the crook a he arm and big black shoes on he foot was before he went to Laventille."

Kaka was Baba younger brother, and I suppose he story is a interesting one although not one I very interested in telling you, except as it come to affect mine and Ganesh life really serious later on. I don't think I qualify to tell Kaka story because I does feel like none a we can't really understand what does make people like Kaka do what they does do, except maybe all the other set a people who do the same thing from all over the country, from Cedros to Mayaro to Sangre Grande and down to Morvant and Laventille.

But I never used to take on what Ganesh say about my own Pa or Baba because sometimes I feel like he didn't understand too good how we used to live with one another in them ten years before he come back for them few days to Four Ways, and while he was talking self, I remember I did think: "And since when you learning learning to fix bones and take away pain, anyhow?" And as we talking now and I thinking back on that time, I thinking about how much none a we coulda foretell what the future will hold, because Ganesh did calling dhoti and kurta schupid until he heself decide that it suit we purpose for him to wear it, and he didn't only put on topi, he put on paghri! But remember, all this come later. Just now I telling you about the time when Ganesh did gone away to Port of Spain and before we did marrid.

As I say, I did like Baba too bad. He was such a tall, good-looking, always happy man with fair fair skin and greyie-greenie eye. But you couldn't see he eyes most a the time because he used to wear big glasses with thick black frame and eyepiece like magnifying glass. Only when he take them off you used to see he eye. I think I must be one a the only people who ever see him without he glasses. He did have thick, white hair and beard and when he eating and he pass the back a he hand to wipe up and clean off he long moustache, you used to see how red he mouth was.

Once he take he walk and done do he work on the estate in the morning and the evening, he used to spend almost he whole day in this same front room reading. He used to siddown by this same desk, next to this same window on this same special chair with these same two arm rest with this cushion on the seat and he used to keep all he books right round on the shelf behind my back here, where he just had to spin round to pick up any book he want. And I suppose when I doing the same thing now, I feeling like it keeping me connect up to him still.

So I didn't use to take on Ganesh when he talking nonsense like that because I did love Baba too bad and I did admire the way he was trying to live and the things he was trying to do. Take this house for instance; you notice the colour a the stainglass window and door? Yes. It green, yellow and white. And is not them colour by mistake, you hear. Them is the colours a the Indian flag. Baba say when he start fixing up this house a couple years after Babu dead, he choose them colours to honour Babu and he own Mai and Babu father and mother who had to leave they home in India because so much thing start to change around them that they didn't know how them and they children woulda survive if they did stay there.

Baba say that Babu tell him that we who born in Trinidad could never imagine how much things did change up in their village in India and force them to leave. He did tell me the name a the village, but I can't remember it no more. He say how people couldn't use the land that them was living on for so much generations and how he family end up with no place to graze their cows, no kinda work in the village, no money to buy thing that they had was to pay for and most a it was things they never have to pay for before and their life just collapse on them.

Baba say that Babu used to tell them this joke about how a set a carpenters in Jalesar hold a big meeting to declare that them is Brahman. They put on janeo and everything. But hear why, nah. They tell the British that they refuse to make theyself impure by working on the rubbish carts for the city, and plenty other workers start following them, not just Jalesar alone, nah, but all over, and India did stinking for months because carpenters did want money for what them did accustom to do for free for generations before. Babu say everybody did have to start to think about money and think about how they could get it, so these carpenter fellas pull that kinda stunt on the authority, who is the ones who teaching them to think in terms a money in the first place.

When Babu father and mother leave to come here, them was hoping to make enough money to go back home to live in this new kinda situation. But they was never able to manage it and they never did imagine that it was so far they coming or what kinda trouble woulda come to them here, and that they would never be able to go back. Now you have to understand, eh, that Baba used to tell we plenty time that he was never one to go around staging rally and demonstration for Indian independence like some other people he did hear about and he never go to no meetings to sing *Vande Mataram* or nothing like that.

He tell me that he never had nothing to do with any a the organisations like the India Club and thing that they did forming in them days, because although he did have a little bit a money from the oil rights and from what the market people used to pay him for what they taking from the farm, he did never have enough money to go back to visit India or to give them for the famine relief fund and thing, which is what them fellas making organisation was doing. He say he just never had the time or the feelings to go and hear any a the Indian missionary or ambassador what he used to read about in the papers or hear people talking about. He say he do what he do with the colours of the doors and windows because he respect how he own father and mother, Babu and Mai, used to talk about their home and how sad they used to feel about how they could never go back.

But is not only big decisions like that that I used to admire Baba for. Was all kinda little things too. Almost every morning he used to go for a walk around the whole village. And sometimes if he going far he used to look like a real hero with he big black shoes, black umbrella and white topi, kurta and dhoti. Most evening, he used to stop by Pa shop for a little bit to talk with all the other men who used to gather up to talk about what happening – all over the

20

world, you know – not just right here in Four Ways.

It had plenty thing to talk about: wars all about, people fighting for independence, religious congress and of course all the little problems people in the village did always have, plenty a which, I telling you, had to with what happening in the rest a the world. Who cow sick. How Mr Ptolemy Sampson, who used to attend to them thing, treat the cow. How much Baboolal charging people to carry them to the train station. How much cane Manwah managing to plant on he piece and how much the factory paying him for it. How much children Mr Chen have now and how much new kinda rum he and he wife Gumlin have in the shop and how much they charging for each kind. What happen to Mr. Perreira and he family since they move outta Four Ways because Perreira get promotion in the oil company and they get a house in the compound. All kinda thing it had to talk about.

Baba was the leader for the direction the talk would take most days. I will never forget one day how he start to explain why he come to meet Pa after Pa threaten the foreman. Baba say that things in these islands have a way a repeating over and over again. And in he opinion, when they make the declaration that every last person who did come here as indenture was finally going to be free a their bondage on the first a January in 1920, not only the estate owners but every single business and factory owner start getting on just like they did get on when they hearing talk that the Queen putting a stop to slavery. Nobody didn't worry about the things that it really had to worry about – like what go happen to the poor people who ain't have no work when first a January come.

Baba say it was a schupid reaction because anybody who was thinking shoulda know that it wasn't going to cause no big change for nobody except for them few sufferers. He say the two things that really was different was Conrad Stollmeyer making kerosene what brighten the darkness without provoking the sleeping spirits a the country, and Walter Darwent drilling the first oil well and changing Trinidad into something nobody didn't dream about before. Baba say both a them make it possible for the war to have enough energy power and that difference was important to understand.

Baba say that because nobody doesn't pay enough attention to these important kinda difference between old times and now, and how these times start putting pressure on people, like them down on the wharf, and that is what cause the dock workers strike. He call plenty names like Huggins, de Verteuil, Bell Smythe, Bowen, McClean, Pasea and plenty others I can't remember any more. Pa used to say that he could never forget the de Verteuil one because it had a de Verteuil who used to come to visit Mr. Lamont in Cedar Grove Estate and Pa say he used to feel very proud to be seeing the man who did own the very first car that come to Trinidad, driving it through the village where he born and grow up. Pa used to say the name a the car like if is something to eat. He used to say it so: "It was a Cadillac steam-powered Locomobile."

But Baba wasn't like Pa and he insist that is them same kinda fellas like de Verteuil that you have to watch close because they know how to keep people quiet by making them look up to them so much. How when they did want to keep the soldiers quiet, they use the same same strategy they did use on people who was getting on for their return passage to go back home to India after their five, eight or ten years a indenture did done. He say the soldiers was coming back home very very angry when the war did done in Europe and wham! just so they settle them up with five acres a land they know was useless and tame them one time. And at the same time, the people who was supposed to get five acres or passage to go back home because they come on that boat in 1917 didn't get nothing, because they did just draw a line across them in India, like if they tell their self, "Eh heh, allyuh want indentureship to done. Well it done. Who catch catch." Baba say that we can't forget that all the big managers and owners a big business in Trinidad did arm their self to the teeth to make sure that if it have trouble because a all a that, them prepared for anything. It stand to reason that the rest a we start to do the same thing, he say, because it eh make no sense to know that the enemy have he guns train on you and you eh arm yourself to put lead in he arse too.

He say is all a that he was thinking when he hear that Pa stand up to the foreman and he come down to the estate to shake the hand of the man who care enough for he dulahin that he willing to buss way somebody gullet to make them pay for what happen to she, no matter what it cost. Baba kinda talk used to make every man jack feel like he ready to be a hero. I used to like to listen to them talk and when people start coming to look for Ganesh to talk in the same way, I used to feel very happy – but I don't mean Beharry, you know. I will tell you more about Beharry later, God rest he soul. He was Ganesh best friend and he and he wife did come like family to we after a time. But when I talking about the people who used to come, I don't mean Beharry because he used to practically live by we. Is when all the other people start coming that I talking about. You know, although Ganesh never talk to me like how Baba used to talk, I did still start to feel like he was fulfilling the destiny Baba did dream of for he when that happen.

When Baba stop going for he walks, it was like a silence descend on the shop and the whole village that nobody didn't want to disturb. Everybody was so frighten.

"Panditji looking sad these days, you hear."

"He does walk so slow now. When I think how he used to step high I does feel so sorry for he," they whispering.

"Hmm. How the mighty are fallen!"

"Bhagwan, you letting the last one a the three brothers, who stay with we and who still remember India like the back a their hand, leave we? Them grandfather come on the boat because they was trying to escape from going to gaol after the mutiny. And after all that trials and tribulations, just so they going to disappear off the face a this land. Prabhu, don't take him yet nah," they praying.

Nobody couldn't bear to think about what it woulda mean for the whole village if he dead. And let me tell you something. When it happen, it was a very big thing. Life change forever for all a we without exception. So, you see, when I used to go on my daily walk up the hill, I was most likely doing it for all a we as much as for me or he. And you know, that is how come Pa let me start to come outside the shop in the evening to talk with the men them, just a handful a them leave back now from the old days when Pa and Ma used to live in the barracks on the Coeur de Jardin Estate. All the others was new people who did move in to Four Ways because a the oil and because it was a good quiet place to live, with electricity, school, standpipe, shop, and nowadays theatre not too far, train, taxi and cartmen – everything anybody coulda need.

Every day I used to tell the people who siddown liming in the evening by the shop what I remember from what Baba say and what he read to me. One day I was telling everybody how Baba was reading *Ramayan* when I went up to visit. I call upstairs when I come through the front door, "Sitaram Baba, Sitaram." He answer back one time, "Come nah, Bayt. I upstairs." I say, "Alright I coming, but I go go up the back step because I bring some bread and I pick one or two mango, mamisipote and orange and I go put them in the kitchen first." When I went in he room, I stoop down and touch he foot and receive he blessings, which is what I used to do whenever I meet him. I never ever forget to do that after Pa bouf me good when I didn't do it the first first time I meet him. Baba close he book and stop he reading one time. He pat me on the head and say Radhayshyam, same way he used to do every time I bow and touch he foot, but this time he say, "You come, Bayt. I glad you come." And he leave he hand on my head for much longer than he accustomed.

Then, when he finally move it and I stand up, he tell me: "You know, Bayti, these days I does think about my son Ganesh too bad. So long me eh see him. I did reading just now how King Dashrath life come to be full a pain and I was wondering about my own. I was that boy mother and father and just like that it come like he disown me. I does wonder sometimes if is because he was too shame when I quarrel with that damn English man what sitting down there in the Principal chair and not even getting up to say good morning to me.

"Me and that man quarrel because I tell him he have to put Ganesh in one a the older boys' class because he coming to school later than them other children and I don't want that to make things difficult for he. And that man watching me like I talking Sanskrit and I know that that is because he ain't want to do what I telling he! I paying the man to help my son get a schooling. I know if they put him with the littler boys it go make him feel like he big and duncy. I telling that man so but he eh want to listen to me. Them does feel that just because we from country, we don't know about them. But since I was a boy I did hear about William Miles and how he does find that what they used to call the free-place boys was lowering the standard a he college and like they make this man in Miles' own image. In he eye, I must be just another one a the hordes a coolies that they shoulda keep behind barricade and not let them come nowhere near the city.

"If Ganesh didn't pull on my sleeve and say soft soft, 'Bap, kuch na bol, don't say nothing, please Bap don't say nothing, nah,' I mighta drop a hand in that Principal arse so hard he woulda see stars. But I eh say or do nothing else because I don't want to make things bad for the boy. After all that, what will happen to Ganesh, Bayti, for treating he father so? That is what I can't stop thinking and I can't sleep when I thinking these things, you know. What I do to have to suffer the way he treating me? I pray my whole life for God to protect me from dvaysh and klaysh and look at how this boy bring down negativity and affliction on my house.

"Raja Dashrath remember why he had to suffer when he sons and daughter-in-law had to leave they comfortable home and go in the forest. He did know that it was because a the curse that Sarwan Kumar father and mother put on he for killing they one son, who was they everything. But what is my curse? Why the boy eh want to come back home? Why he don't want to get marrid to the girl I choose for he? What it have in town that better than becoming a man and making a family? Sarwan Kumar father and mother give up their life because they couldn't live after he dead, but in my case my Kumar give me up for dead and I think maybe is time for me to grant him he wish."

When he say that, I start to cry. I say, "Baba please don't talk so. I sure Ganesh ain't give you up for dead. He must be just trying to make a way for he self. He must be trying to become a man on he own strength." But Baba didn't want to hear none a that. He say, "But what schupidness is that, Bayti? A person can't come a man by their self. They have to do that with a family. Is the family does teach a man how to be a man. Is the family position in the village that does make that family a family that will be remembered through all the days of that village and give the village a position in the country. Is because so much people forget this that we had to leave India and run. Babu say up to the day he dead that he Baba used to remember and cry about how they end up landless and homeless because everybody did want they own mahal. Everybody did want money instead a the grains they used to share among theyself before.

"It come a time when that wasn't a bad thing because it didn't have too much grain, but it didn't have no money neither. And by that time people didn't care who they had to throw in a gutter to get money. That is what make Babu father join the freedom fighters in India, and then when they lost and the British start to hunt them down and kill them off or throw them in jail and throw way the key, then he had to grab he poor wife and they three sons and run like hell, not knowing where he going to go with them to get them to a safe place. I don't think he did know what he going to do at all. Ganesh throw me in a gutter just like them people what we leave behind and run from, and I can't fight my own son."

While I was still suskaying and wiping my nose quick quick with the back of my hand quiet quiet, so he wouldn't see or hear because I could see how much he in pain, he stand up and come closer to me. He pass he hand over my head and he say, "But look at what I doing to my Bayti. Don't worry about what I just say. Come leh we go in the kitchen and we go have some of them hops bread you just bring and a cup a hot Milo and both of we will feel better and I will stop thinking about Ganesh and he foolishness."

And just as I finishing tell the people liming by the shop what he say at his house, Baba walk up to we there. I laugh and cover my mouth with my two hand and start to run to him, saying, "Baba, you catch me telling a story about you." But before I could reach him, Ramanand who did sitting down on the last step and who get up to greet him, say in a sharp voice, "Panditji, you alright?" Before the words was out he mouth good, he reach out and hold up Baba, who was collapsing right there in front a we eye just so, just so. It was that simple. He just fall, and like while Ramanand holding he body from reaching the ground, the life did done gone. I don't know if it was hearing he own story repeat back to him or what. You know how they say that the day somebody sing the story a your own life back to you, you will know that the end a your road near? Well I don't know if is that or what, but just so he gone.

Pa shout at me, "Girl, go quick and put some tulsi in a cup a water and bring it come." When I come with it, Pa make me take a spoon and put a little bit in Baba mouth. I was crying and crying but even I self admiring how he looking like a king where Ramanand rest him down on the sheet what Pa make me spread on the ground. He was lying down there with he white hair and beard, white jersey and dhoti that always leave he ankle and calves showing and he black shoes and he did smiling and looking peaceful like if he just close he eye for a minute.

Pa make Ramanand and some other men pick up the sheet from the four corners and the middle on each side. They even let Boysie help out. Boysie used to catch malkadi sometimes and nobody didn't use to treat him like the other young people in the village and give him little jobs to do and thing because a that. But it was such a blessing to get the chance to carry that man body that everybody make a space for Boysie and all a them close in on the body and all a we walk behind them up the hill and when we reach here they put him down in the drawing room in front so.

Doolarie Mausi start to sing *Krishen, Kanha, Manohar, Mukunda* and all a we start chanting after she. They rest down the body on the floor as soon we get inside the house, with the head facing north and the foot facing the door. We light a deeya by the head. Then Utme Chachi tie a piece a cloth around he face – under the chin with the knot on top a he head. You don't ever see them thing again, eh? People don't do them things now because the body does go straight in the funeral home after the person dead. But so we used to do it long time. Then Chachi tie he thumbs together and he big toes. And then we take down the pictures in the house and put them away and cover all the mirrors with cloth. After that, the men them take over the body to wash it and dress it and we went outside and continue to sing.

So while we doing that, Pa and all the villagers start to make arrangements for the funeral. Pa send Moean Chacha to tell Pandit Dan and Ramdass Mamu, who was the ones who used to do puja and nau work for all the three brothers until Kaka move up Laventille and stop doing puja. He ask Balwant to go and arrange for the boys to cut bamboo and coconut branch the next day to make a tent. He give Bhola the job to go and ask Theophilus if he go make arrangements for the grave and bring over one a he best coffins. And he ask Manohar to go by the doctor house on the estate to ask him to see about getting the death certificate and to make sure and tell the man how sorry he is to disturb him that hour a the evening.

Pa fix up everything and then he turn to me and say, "Now for the most important part. We have to let Ganesh know. Panditji did say that Ganesh living by one Mrs Cooper on Dundonald Street in Port of Spain. We have to go in the Post Office and get them to send off a telegram for he. You go have to write it out for me, Leela, and Vishnu and me will go and send it off. Now the thing with telegram is you have to say what you have to say in a very little bit a words, because every letter count. What you go say?" I run inside one time and I get a pencil and write on a piece a paper something so: 'Bad. news. come. home. now.' Pa take the paper and put it in he pocket and Vishnu come with he old beat-up Ford; I can't remember the numbers a none of the cars we had in we life, but I never forget the number of that car – P 435. Vishnu did buy it from the doctor on the estate; and he and Pa went in it to send off the telegram.

After we was just marrid, Ganesh say to me one time, "It funny eh. Look at me. Marrid to a Ramlogan and just yesterday I did asking, who is this Ramlogan who sign this telegram telling me I must come now?" Later on, he used to grumble that from the time the Ramlogans come into he life, they start telling him what to do. Truth was, when we did just marrid he was a little more confused about how just so just so he whole life was about doing what we tell him to do. We make him, you know, into what he become before he leave Trinidad and Tobago, which is what a wife and she family does always do for she husband.

People used to be saying, "Who the hell is this Ganesh?" But the more useful question woulda be, "Who the hell is this Leela?" Perhaps by the time you done write your book they will realise that that is the proper question and I hope you give them all the answers they need. If they think Ganesh is a rishi, they should know that the rishi wife always more important than he, never mind how long or short a time she play that role for him. Maybe Ganesh and all will realise that and know that he should be thankful for it.

CHAPTER 2: A TURNING POINT: GANESHJI, MY HUSBAND-TO-BE

Everybody in this country does remember Ganesh as a great statesman from the 1940s and 50s. That is not my main memory. Mostly I does remember the 23-years old young man who come back to Four Ways frighten and confused about who he was, now that he father gone. He musta been wondering exactly what he future would be. When I used to dress like Doris Day after he become the grand statesmen, sometimes I used to sing *Que Sera Sera* quiet quiet to myself and think about that night so long ago and how he face was so dark and how the darkness a the night hide the greenie-grey and give him dark eyes too.

I see him for the first time that night and didn't want to stop looking at him ever after – except for a few days a long time ago when I thought that life was giving me a big chance for my best life, without he in it. When I first see him, I was thinking that Ganesh must be resemble he mother, because he eh look nothing like Baba. He was the opposite a Baba in every way except for the eyes, but for some reason I find that make him even more handsome than Baba. Maybe because a the black skin, he eyes used to blaze in he face, although in shape and colour, complete with the long curly eyelashes, they was exactly like Baba one.

But it take me a long time to realise the sameness. You know, if I coulda still do it, I wouldn't want nothing more even now in these last days than to siddown right here in this same house and look at Ganesh reading. But it too late to think about that now. He gone where he did think he truly belong and since I couldn't agree with him on that, I stay here where I feel I belong, in he father house. Maybe he finally realise now that this is where he and he family belong too, in which case is me who go have to mash land. But we go have to wait and see about that one.

So, as I say, Ganesh come back for he father funeral. You know, people who talk about Baba funeral say he was cremated. He wasn't cremated. I telling you! Rumours have a way a growing right in front a your eyes until they become a reality that nobody wouldn't dream to doubt. But is not true. Not even my own father did get the chance for he body to get offer in the fire. Only Phua manage to be so lucky. You see, that time we couldn't cremate we dead, so Baba bury in Four Ways Public Burial Grounds according to the regulations set out in the Burial Grounds Act. The cremation act didn't pass until 1953. In fact, it was one a the most important things that Ganesh help people to achieve in this country and one a the last things he get a chance to do too before trouble come looking for we and make him absent from my life for good.

In death, Baba compete with everything he have, just like how he used to compete in life and the place a he burial still mark by the best architecture in any cemetery on this island. When Bhola went to ask Theophilus if he will get the coffin and the grave ready, Theophilus tell him that he was waiting on somebody to come and put them question to him for quite a few days, because Baba did done come to see him to choose he coffin and pay him for the job, and after that they siddown together and design the mausoleum that Baba did want Theophilus to build on top a the grave afterwards.

Sometimes I does still go and sit down there and talk to him a little bit, especially when the Local Government Minister make sure the cemetery clean for All Souls Day. Let we go and I will show you where it is and how pleasant it is to siddown in the shade a the giant mausoleum with the smell a the pink frangipani growing next to it fulling up your nose, the birds whistling fulling up your ears and butterflies floating from flower to flower fulling your eye with gladness to be alive in the grounds a the dead, who share them same feelings while they walk above where their bodies resting now.

Sometimes I does think that how I feel about Baba must be have plenty to do with how I come to feel and care about he son. Baba tell me that he did make plans to get Ganesh marrid to Bhagwandass daughter. Baba woulda check patra to make sure gana baithé and thing to make that decision, but nobody else wasn't thinking about that. Everybody know how rich Bhagwandass is and how much he only daughter did stand to inherit from she father and how much a son-in-law woulda possess in that case. Knowing that Ganesh refuse to get marrid to she make me look at him in a certain way when he come back home, and right through the wake and the funeral I was just watching him, thinking what kind a man woulda do something so. So even when Pandit Dan command we to sing, I just watching him, even though I open my mouth and I singing:

Koyi na lejai hai
Dhan bandh ke gathariya

Jab yamraja palanga par baithe
Ulata gaye dono naina patariya

Koyi na lejai hai
Dhan bandh ke gathariya

Marihi soota prana nikale
Prana lokayi kothariya kothariya

Koyi na lejai hai
Dhan bandh ke gathariya

Char prahar mile kata uthawe
Phuka deeya jaise banke lakariya

Koyi na lejai hai
Dhan bandh ke gathariya

Kahat Kabir suno bhayee sadhu
Chhuti jaye sab mahal utariya

Koyi na lejai hai
Dhan bandh ke gathariya

You really don't hear them kinda bhajan again. You right. Is the sadness a that kinda bhajan what cause me to think so much about how Baba grieve to see Ganesh before he dead. Same time I watching him, I was feeling afraid a this man with the blazing eyes who coulda do such a thing to he own father. But I also thinking that when we tell him that he have to keep the light lighting by Baba head, he do it, and that is a hard thing to do because almost every hour you have to go and full up the deeya with oil. And if the spirit travelling fast, and I sure Baba one must be was speeding, the deeya does burn out much much faster than that. So is a kinda – what you does call it? – a vigil you does have to keep to make sure the light keep lighting. And then I thinking that I did hear about the trouble he make for he janeo to shave he head, and I was expecting the same thing for the funeral, but Ganesh let them shave he head without making no fuss and he do everything Pandit Dan and Pa tell him to do very very obedient.

Later, of course, I did realise is just schupid Ganesh schupid and he break Baba heart outta just dotishness. Ganesh did like to call people baklol sadhu, but very often I think that he was the biggest baklol in plenty situation. But that night something a the fright I develop from watching Baba grieve did affect the way I did looking at Ganesh. I think Pa see me looking at him in a kinda close way and after the funeral, Pa start to find ways a making Ganesh look back at me, because maybe he didn't understand all what making me look. For two months, Pa courtening Ganesh for me, calling him Ganeshji and thing, and I thinking things woulda go on so for the year until we do the final bhandara for Baba. But I was wrong. First first, Pa start to send me with all the things I used to carry for Baba for Ganesh. Thank God I never meet Ganesh home, and I was kinda glad every time it happen – or didn't happen would be a better way to say it.

As soon as the funeral done, Ganesh start roaming around the place, not talking to nobody, like how Baba used to do, not even looking at them straight in their eye self. Just walking about doing nothing in particular. Ganesh bounce up with another one who I did fraid that time, just as much as I fraid Ganesh. He was a white Scotsman who everybody call Mr Stewart. He did come to live in one a the Coeur de Jardin estate house a few months before

Ganesh come back and sometimes you used to see the two a them walking and talking together. Baba did say one time that Mr Stewart is one a them people that other white people don't like too much because he gone native. I think that is because Stewart used to dress sometimes like a sadhu or a wali in a gown, something like a very long kurtah.

And then one day, as soon as the shaving and bhandara done, we see Ganesh coming up the hill riding on a new three-speed bike. Afterwards, he proudly tell Pa he buy the bicycle from Daniel's Bicycle Shop on Coffee Street. It was the best shop where everybody in Four Ways used to go to buy their bicycle if they coulda ever manage to afford to buy a new one, so everybody know that shop. Well, after he get that bike, is like he making up for years a he childhood what he did lost in town. Ganesh used to go riding all over the place. People used to see him sometimes quite down the road heading Princes Town side. Sometimes they even see him heading Debe side. So when Pa send me with something I used to be glad if I meet Shairoon Chachi. I used to just give the goods to she and if she not there I used to just go up the back step and put down whatever Pa send for he in the kitchen and then go back home. Sometimes I used to pass by the burial ground to tell Baba what going on and what Ganesh doing since he come home.

And Pa used to look out for when Ganesh riding in front the shop and he used to call him to come in. Pa used to like to hear him talk because when you go to town school, you does learn to talk different, like if you come from foreign, like some a the estate manager and overseer and them. Every time Pa trying to get him to sit down so that he could get a chance to bring up my name, I used to catch a fit a giggles. But Pa is not a man who does give up just so, and by the time he done with Ganesh, Ganesh was coming every day and eating by we, and agreeing to all the arrangements for a wedding which Pa decide was going to be "a proper three weeks' affair", which is the exact words Pa say. I was peeping and watching them talking, and I hearing Ganesh protesting that he didn't see the sense in that at all because it have a proper time to do everything. And he ask Pa if they shouldn't pay some mind to that and ask Pandit Dan for advice. But Pa say he eh think that necessary.

So you have to understand, eh, that most a this proper was Pa own sense of proper, not nobody else one. For me, the best proper woulda be if we did wait for the year to pass and Baba bhandara done before we even start talking about wedding and courtening and thing, and I think that that is what Ganesh did think too, even though I never ask him. I didn't have much to say about what going on at all, and even when I try sometimes to say what I thinking, nobody taking me on, not even Soomintra Didi who maybe was just worried that she go have to come Four Ways to help out for the wedding.

Things start properly in Pa eye when he ask Ganesh what he going to do in the future. That day, when Ganesh come in the shop, Pa did hand him a book to look at from a set he did just buy a few days before from one a the people who used to drive around selling books and thing. Pa do that just to impress Ganesh, I sure. Ganesh raise the book in he right hand and say very serious-like, in a voice just like the one he use when he put he hand on the Bible when he get called to be the statesman, "I going to be a author of books like these." Well, Pa laugh one a the happiest laugh I ever hear he laugh and he make Ganesh siddown, and right away them start to make wedding plans.

Them decide that they going to get modern cards for the wedding instead a sending the nau with the saffron rice neota to invite everybody. That was the first big mistake the two a them make because it take away from one family in we own village the right them did always have to play their own special role in a wedding. So properly for them was when Ganesh siddown and design a card neither a them couldn't understand, instead a allowing Ramdass Mamu and he family to perform the duty that they doing for everybody else in the village from childbirth to death. When trouble come afterwards, I think that that was one a the wrong doings that cause it.

Thing like that could cause plenty bacchanal. I remember one time that Ramdass Mamu say that the right to massage people was he one and Baba self didn't have no right to be doing that job. But Pa and Ganesh didn't think for a minute that other people woulda be watching what they doing, and that what they was doing was really changing everything forever. So people talk. Thank God they still let Ramdass Mamu and he wife do the nau work for the puja part, and let Ramdass Mamu family-self supply all the soharie leaf for people to eat on. They let them decorate the tent and the car and everything when the wedding time come, just like they did always do for everybody else.

'Properly', after they done design the card, was to go and get the card print quite in San Fernando. After that 'properly' was when a set a people dress up in their Sunday best come down from Baba house to we house behind Vishnu motorcar what have a speaker on it playing music. They bring the gifts to ask for me to get marrid to Ganesh. Pa look very happy and agree very seriously to take part in he own gift-giving of kanyadan. The only good part a that whole thing is that it was the first time I get a chance to talk to Fyzabad Phua, although I was seeing she from far ever since she move into Baba house when she come for he funeral. I did see she plenty times before that when she come to visit Baba and he first tell me who she is one day when I was a little girl. I was playing school and beating all the house pillars with a stick for not doing their homework under the house.

Baba put he hand around she shoulder and say, "This is my own Didi, Bayti." And then he tell she that I is he bayti who come to keep him company now that Ganesh not there. He turn back to me and say, "So you could call she Fyzabad Phua just like how Ganesh does do." I used to like to watch how she and Baba was with one another whenever they meet. They used to hug up each other and start talking fast fast and laughing about what they saying in a language that used to sound just like what the pandits does use in puja and all a we does use when we singing songs like the ones we sing for Baba funeral. I don't always understand that language too good, except sometimes when I repeat what some-body say over and over in my mind to try and figure it out.

Fyzabad Phua take the gifts after the men pass them around from one to the next and then she tell Pa to call the girl. When I come, she say, "Bayti, let me put these things on for you. The last lady who wear them was Ganesh mother and she would be too glad to see them on you." Looking at she was like looking at a lady Baba, same fair skin, same greenie eye, same white hair, same soft smile and gentle face, but no glasses. When she done pin on the jewels, she put a big bag in my hand and say, "This is what you will put on when you done bathe on the wedding Sunday." She was the only real thing for me that day because I didn't feel like she was a part a the 'properly' that Ganesh and Pa was doing.

The next weekend we had matikor on the Friday evening, cooking night on the Saturday, and then Sunday morning the wedding start. The Harischandra dancers sing and dance whole night on the Saturday while the cooking taking place and that was probably a very nice part for everybody. I did see them perform only one time before when Gauri Aji did find oil in she piece and she did have a nine-night yagya in thanks. They did dance on the last night of the yagya and I remember nobody didn't come home until after midnight.

Almost all the children from CM school used to go to the yagya every night, and me, Shareeda, Rehana, Soomintra Didi, Jacqueline and Marguerite was very pleased with weself to be walking up the road to come home so late in the night. Jacqueline and Marguerite was Mr Theophilus' daughters. Jacqueline used to go every night. She still living Four Ways and does do puja and thing all the time because when she went in mourning, Hanuman Baba appear to she, but Marguerite used to just go because she like parsad and that night nobody couldn't stop she from going to that good show.

Moti Kaki did also do the same thing when she start getting some oil money from she own land and all. But she did have the Indrasabha on the last night a she one, and that was a next one that people couldn't done talk about for a long time afterwards. The Harischandra and the Indrasabha people was professional people, you see, not ordinary people who playing a part like what does happen for Ramlila or Hosay and thing. So seeing them was very exciting for all a we, although I didn't really get to mix on the cooking night for my own wedding because I did have to stay inside.

Still, come to think of it, the Harischandra was really a nice part a the whole wedding and it show me how much Pa wanted to do thing in style for me. So I was alright after that, right up to the next morning when the little girls was putting on the hardi during the puja, and I was still alright when the bigger girls, who did just get marrid, was taking it off with dahee in the bathroom afterwards. It was plenty laughing and joking between them about how I going to find out soon why all a them fat and happy and why they smoothening and softening me up so that I could be just like them. They tease me about how I is just skin and bones but that Ganesh will soon make me round out all about. After that they send me to bathe and when I finish bathe, before I could dry up myself, Ramdass Mami bring a bucket of soapy-looking water and tell me that I have to throw that on me last thing before I dry off. When I ask she what it is, she say is the water what run off from Ganesh skin when he was bathing.

I don't know how I didn't know they would a make me do that. It must be happen at all the hundreds a other people wedding I went to but I don't know how I never realise. That did make me frighten because I thinking I don't know what I doing and what people expecting from me, and I all alone and it eh have nobody I could talk to, to tell them how I feeling. And then I thinking that I not throwing that man nasty run-off water on my clean skin. I throw it away but with a loud splash so it sound like if it falling normal. I raise up the bucket high over my head and throw it far from me to the other side a the bathroom and then I open the door a little bit and hand back Ramdass Mami the bucket without saying a word.

By the time I went inside to dress and I hearing the ladies singing the Sunday morning lawa songs, I did start to tremble real bad and it wasn't because the water I did just bathe in was cold. I thinking about how I eh have no mother to be with me. Even though Soomintra Didi trying she best, I never let she feel she could mother me because she too bossy, and if you did let she get she own way even once self, she woulda take over your whole life and run it like a factory. She didn't use to be so bad. She really get so after she get marrid. So I was by myself when the ladies start to sing the lawa songs because I tell she that I don't need nobody to help me to put on some clothes when I doing that for myself my whole life.

Is the songs what make me think about what I doing, getting marrid to this man who make Baba cry – and so soon after Baba dead. You not supposed to cry for the dead because your tears does fall on them and burn like acid and you not supposed to celebrate neither. So, I thinking this is a sure sign a disrespect for the dead and something bad woulda happen. But even so, I did love to dance and sing the lawa songs and if you did ask me that morning, I woulda tell you I really don't know how come I crying when I hearing the ladies singing:

Mor lawa Tor lawa
Eke may milay day

Mor bhowji Tor bhaiya
Eke may sutay day

Mor lawa Tor lawa
Eke may milay day

Mor bhowji Tor bhaiya
Eke may sutay day

Mor lawa Tor lawa
Eke may milay day

Mor bhateeji Tor bhateeja
Eke may sutay day

Mor lawa Tor lawa
Eke may milaay day

And then the tassa start beating and I thinking just now the sindoor will lagaye on me and still I crying, when at anybody else wedding I woulda be laughing and dancing. I coulda follow the steps a all the fellas who laughing and dancing like ladies and giving their special blessing in exchange for money from the dulaha and dulahin fathers. Even as I crying, I remembering how I did dance for Soomintra Didi wedding and how Pa did get drunk after the wedding leave because he was so happy. Then I remember how Didi did cry too until she see how happy Pa was. Then I start to feel a little better because I think how happy Pa must be feeling. When Ganga Aji, who play mother-part, come for me, I don't think she woulda see that I did crying just a few minutes before. It did help me plenty to think about how happy and pleased with heself Pa must be feeling.

"Saubhaagyavati Bhava," Pandit Dan say, as he shower he blessings on me when I bow to touch he and Ganesh foot when the wedding done that night and Ganga Aji was going to carry me back inside. But when he say that, I start to shiver again, like if somebody walk over my grave. Maybe I was feeling so because a the way my nerves did so wrack since this whole business start on the day I was telling back Baba *Ramayan* story to the people in front a the shop.

Inside, I change my clothes and put on the nice dress Soomintra Didi buy in San Fernando for me. She say is what they does call the going-away dress and all brides does do that now. They don't just go in the same sari they get marrid in, like how they did make she do. Then I call Ganga Aji and she come and carry me back outside. With the tassa playing and the mike playing harder and everybody throwing rice and flowers on we as we walking from the house to get in Vishnu car – what dress up with flowers and shiny paper – me and Ganesh come up here to Baba house. Fyzabad Phua come and meet we by the car. She and a set a other ladies do we aarti and carry we by the kohobar for the final ceremonies and then the wedding did finally done.

I was so tired that when she show me where me and my lokni will sleep in one corner a the drawing room with a whole set a other woman and children sleeping all over the place, it look like as soon as I just siddown on the khatiya, I fall asleep one time. When I wake up in the morning I did still have on the dress what was Soomintra Didi wedding present. It look like somebody take off my shoes and put me to lie down properly while I was sleeping, which was the only good 'properly' anybody did do for me in a long time. Ganesh sleep where he used to always sleep in this house, which is a room I did never see until I move back here and start to sleep in it by myself.

I was well glad, you hear, when Pa and a group a people he arrange from we side come back with music on the Wednesday and carry me back home. The next Sunday, Ganesh and he side wedding party was supposed to come back again. They was supposed to come to take me back to Baba house for we to begin we life as normal. But one set a ruction take place after I come back on the Wednesday and the way things end up wasn't very proper, which is what I sensing was going to happen all along, because everybody pick up with some kinda crazy speed after Baba dead and the end a that kinda speed couldn't be nothing but trouble.

Is Kaka from Laventille what arrive on the scene that bring the trouble. First time I see he. I did only ever hear about him before. He never come for Dada funeral. He never come for Dadi funeral. He never come for Baba funeral. But he saying that oh he get to find out that Ganesh getting marrid and he had to come to see we. He stop by the shop first, he say, because he thought that Dookhie did still there and he meet Pa instead. I was inside but I could see and hear plain what going on.

Ganesh well accustom to eating by we every day, and although Pa try to do things properly and thought Ganesh woulda eat home, now that it have so much so much different woman living in he house and cooking, he still used to come to eat during the wedding time, when by all rights he shoulda stop. That day he come soon after Kaka reach and he meet him talking to Pa. Pa turn to Ganesh, but before he coulda finish ask Ganesh why he don't let Kaka stay with he in he father house, even though it have all the ladies there, because, after all, Kaka is he family too, I shock to hear Ganesh saying in a very disgusted kinda way I never expect to hear from him, "What the hell you doing here, man? Like you feel you could come here and make my life hell like how you did make Bap and Dada life hell?"

I was even more shock when Kaka answer, "Don't talk to me so, boy. I come here to give you notice that you and all the people I hearing and seeing you have here better vacate my property before I get the bailiff to throw allyuh out." Ganesh look like he rush at Kaka and Pa like he try to come between them. Pa was on the ground, with the two a them on top him, when I come out in the shop to try to put a stop to everything before somebody kill somebody. I start to bawl for help when I realise I couldn't handle it by myself, and Sonachan, who was passing in the road, come inside quick and make out what going on right away and help me to separate them. All this time, Ganesh still shouting from where Sonachan kinda corner him, "You and who getting me to leave my father house?"

Is then Kaka pull out a thick stack a paper from he pocket, push it towards Ganesh and say, "The Governor General and me." Ganesh reach for the paper and Sonachan take it from Kaka and pass it to he. Ganesh face get pale and he sit down on a bench one time like he fraid he going to fall. Pa take the paper from he hand when Ganesh ain't saying nothing and Pa start whispering and knocking the back a he fingers on the paper, "But what is this? What is this? But I understanding right? This paper saying he have control a the whole thirty-four-acre block? The whole thing what we thinking Baba and Dada leave for you, and more besides!"

Kaka laugh then and say, "I glad allyuh understand. I come back to say I don't want nobody on my property unless they paying me the rent I asking for." Ganesh get up and say, and maybe he was doing that on Pa behalf eh, "You ever hear occupiers have rights?" Kaka eh look surprise by the question. He just laugh again and say, "I know. You eh see I come alone just to tell allyuh what going to happen. When I come back in six weeks' time from this first notice, I will inform allyuh what the terms a any future occupation going to be." And with that he walk out and everything turn dead and silent behind him.

So you see what happen to my life, right? I can't help thinking that because my father did so hurry to make all arrangements for wedding, so that he could get me off he hand, he end up putting me in shit street. But maybe I shouldn't be so hard on him. Maybe he did want to do he duty to the best a he ability for he children, for who he had to be mother and father after Ma dead. But that is how Pa end up giving Ganesh the place in Fuente Grove that he did get from a man who did owing he plenty money for a bill Pa let him run up, knowing full well that if he can't pay in cash he could get him to pay in kind with the house and the plot a land that Pa did know he own.

Pa do that same thing with plenty fellas who was drinkers, and that is how he did come to own one or two properties in the ten years since we leave the barracks. I hear how Pa and this man went to the Red House with the man house deed and Pa say they just had to ask for a man name Robert James Charles and tell him they come to do a transfer for a property and wait outside for he to come back with the new deed. Them say Pa give this Charles some money for he service and come back home a new home-owner. People say after the wedding that *Oh, Ganesh trick Pa in the kitcheree into giving away he house and land*. One man make up a whole story about how Ganesh siddown like a overdressed Buddha and refuse to eat and cause Pa to shell outta set a money as well as house and land and cows. But is not so it go. What happen happen because a Kaka. After Kaka leave and things get a little quiet, Pa tell Ganesh to go home and sleep and they will work out something the next day. I wasn't parta the conversation them had. Pa tell me afterwards what they decide.

On the Sunday, instead a going to Baba house, which I thought I woulda be doing, we went Fuente Grove instead. Pa give we a cow too when we was leaving, because I feel he was worried like hell about how we go live now that the $60.00 a month rent was going to go to Kaka and not to Ganesh. Is not so it happen after all, but we didn't know that then. Pa even put some money in my hand when we leaving, even though he know Ganesh had the biscuit pan full up with the money from the kitcheree, and is he who pay for the taxi before we pull out. He remind the two a we that he going to stay right there in that shop and deal with Kaka whenever he come back to make more trouble. He send the cow and the one or two other things that had to go Fuente Grove from Four Ways in a cart afterwards, and he pay for that too.

So I hope that is one correction we could make in what people think them know about we. Is Kaka work that things turn out the way they happen. It take so much years a lawyer fee in what we was thinking was a court battle. That is a thing everybody in this country does talk about in whispers because they fraid it so much. We spend almost we whole marrid life under the fear a this court battle against Kaka. Is only almost at the end a things that Ganesh come to understand that nobody could take away from him something that was he own by right. But by that time like he heart did break and he never come back, not once self, to this house ever again. In the meantime, the nastiness that cause Kaka to do what he do to we, lead him to make all kinda other trouble like that, and every time against he own own family.

The most painful and shameful story we get to hear about was when the American soldiers did come down and Kaki start to make fares from them. I didn't even know what that mean until we neighbour explain it for me. You know, I never know she real name up to now, because everybody used to just call she Suruj Mooma and outta respect I call she Beharry Bhowji, so I can't even tell you exactly the name of the person who I talking about. Kaka used to beat Kaki, I hear, when he start to get she to go make fares, and she try to say she not going to do it. I hear that start to happen in 1941 when things did just start to pick up in we own life. But I never really like to listen to gossip like that because I see plenty life get ruin with gossip that way. I only saying what I hear now to show you the kinda man Kaka was and to say that if thing happen so with Kaki, then I very very sorry for she. Nobody and especially no woman should have to put up with anybody touching them in any way when they don't want that to happen. If that was Kaki fate, then it was one that might cause she, poor thing, to want to hunt down Kaka over many lifetimes to get the justice that she must be dead longing for. I see the terror what Kaka did cause to Ganesh, so I can't even begin to imagine how much more thousand times worse it must be affect Kaki.

People don't talk about Kaka and Kaki no more, thank God, but I feel that that is what cause none a their children to stay with them. Every single one went away to England. Kaki dead soon after the war, in 1945 self, but we didn't hear about it until afterwards and we don't know how it happen. I woulda like to meet she. People in Four Ways who did know she used to talk about she as one a the most beautiful woman they ever clap their eye on. God alone know how she dead, and after the case did done when Kapildev finally explain things and put the case behind Ganesh for good, we hear Kaka end up in a poor house on Nelson Street, Port-a-Spain.

Kaka ten-acre piece what bounding we twenty-four on the southern side is still a worry these days. It done get mash up with the drilling and now something else happening. Since marijuana not legal no more, not like long time when I was a little girl and the fellas used to take their toke normal normal in front-a the shop, now we hearing how fellas who not from we village clear a couple acres in the middle a Kaka piece and they planting it there. We have red riyo plant on the boundary line but because a that I don't even go near the riyo line self, far more to cross it.

I does think, eh, that nobody ever benefit in any way from anything Kaka ever had or Kaka ever do. In fact, is the very opposite that happen and that is a hell of a sad life to live. What even worse is that he show heself to be a very foolish man, not worthy a being Babu son and Baba brother because he actions mean that he done book so many many more sadder lives for heself in the future because a what he do in this one. But I don't want to think or talk about he anymore. I just hope I never have to meet him or come anywhere close to where he have to exist in any one a he other lives. I wish that he was just a stranger what we did owe something to and that he don't really belong to Babu lineage and that payment for whatever we did owe done make in this lifetime and nobody will ever have to ever meet up with he again.

CHAPTER 3: FUENTE GROVE

Ganesh put on a brave face whole road while we going Fuente Grove and telling me how excited he feeling to start a life in this new place with me. "In this place that name after fountains," he say, "we will be very happy because it must be a paradise in truth." I trying to trust what he saying, but my mind not easy, wasn't easy since the day I telling back the *Ramayan* story and Baba fall down and never get back up. And then I realise as soon as we reach in that hot, dry, hard place that if we want paradise, the only way to get it woulda be to create it for we self.

While we was driving up and down, up and down the hills and hollows, through the miles and miles a cane between here and there, I did keep my fingers cross that we woulda come out into a nice little village where people take nothing and make something outta it like we did do in Four Ways. As it turn out, I did hoping wrong, and even when we try we couldn't make paradise for a very long time, and when finally we do manage to do it, it wasn't only for we self that we did do it, but for everybody, which, of course, is the right way for people to do thing.

But it take a long time before we make a alternative to the only fountain the people used to drink from in that place. That was the one in Beharry shop that Beharry heself, who wasn't like Pa at all, although the two a them was shopkeeper, was smart enough never to drink from. Even though he from a outta the way place like Fuente Grove, he was smart enough to go and get the license that he need to let him have a rum shop and put up the sign for he fountain a spirituous liquors. Beharry was a smart man in more ways than one. He was smart enough to always put he wife in front a he like a shield, and that poor woman who he have making child after child, year after year, just like my schupid sister

45

Soomintra, didn't object not once in my hearing. If I did ever have children, I would a end up big and fat like the two a them. But I remain nice and slim and able to wear Doris Day dresses as long as Ganesh require me to wear them, which is the position to which life in Fuente Grove eventually lead both a we. Many years pass before that day, though. And long before that I learn to be a seamstress, so that I did know how to get the Doris Day dresses when the time come.

But I only start to think that way long long afterwards. When I was a little girl I never think about *if* I go have children, it was always *when* I go have children and I used to think I woulda have plenty, more than Beharry Bhowji or Soomintra Didi. But after we was living in Fuente Grove for a whole year I start to think that it have something in that place that drying me out, just like it dry out the place. Something like it blocking up all the springs in the land and none a we living there didn't know how to find them.

I ask Pa if he know anybody who woulda know how to find them, but he say it was Baba father, Babu, who did find the ones that the people in Four Ways does still use to bathe and water their animals and plants. And plenty people does still use the water from the springs for cooking and drinking because they still don't trust the water in the standpipes that the government put up in Four Ways. Only a few people who living on the estate compound did have pipe run to bring water right inside their house, like how Baba do here from ever since with water from the spring near to the house. People didn't used to like the standpipe much because some people did start to bathe right there and them feel like the water not clean enough to drink or use to cook.

But nobody Pa know coulda remember how people used to find spring long time. Pa ask me if I could see any seep a water anywhere in the ground, because that mighta help to find the spring that it might be coming from, if it have any. But in all the years I walking about the place, I never find a single seep. We used to have to catch rainwater in barrel what Pa get from the oil company and send up for me, and in dry season I used to have to go by the well on the estate boundary to full back up the barrels bucket by bucket. We didn't have no idea how to make the place come to life until Ganesh come mystic many many years after we reach there.

When we reach Fuente Grove, as far as I could see, the one mango tree in that whole village was in the yard in front a the house we was going to live in. It was the only sign a hope in that whole place, no matter how far I walk. But even that mango prove to be false because it cause a lotta work for me and it didn't, as I expecting from the labour I put into it, help any a the flowers plants I try to grow in the yard. I did just want to have a few flowers to do puja. But, from early in the morning, I have to be sweeping up the leaves what fall from that tree and it never bear a single mango, not once self.

Up to now I don't know what kinda mango tree it was. I feel it must be one a them hybrid variety they was experimenting on when the government farm did start up a project to diversify agriculture and ship mango overseas. Plenty new mango come from that time – Saibani, Governor, Calabash, Rose, Julie – plenty plenty that people don't even remember that they didn't used to exist before that time. But I don't know what kind that was growing in the yard because it never bear nothing. It was big, tall and broad like a old Vert or Sou Sen Matin but since I not sure, I did give it the name "Fuente Harden Tree". Allyuh ever learn that song:

Mango vere, mango teen
Mango vere, mango teen
I want a penny to buy mango vere, mango teen
Mango doux-doux, sou sen matin
Savez-vous all for me.

I feel that might be a good way to remember what was what. The names that not in the song didn't used to exist before the experiment start.

None a the flowers I trying to plant didn't catch, not even hibiscus or ixora or pride a Barbados and them is the kinda flowers plant that if you just chook a stick from another plant in the ground in Four Ways, a new one used to grow. I still try and try, eh, even when I see that the leaves I mixing with manure and piling up around the roots not helping. As for the bhaji and ochro and peas I try my hand at, that did give me plenty more trouble.

I used to have to put in more labour on them thing than if I did have a child. And you think Ganesh care? No! The only thing I could remember about him in all a that time is when he leave me with my mouth open one day, when he declare something so outta the blue to nobody in particular, because he wasn't watching me when he was saying it. He saying, like he reading a book, "Trinidad and Tobago is located 10 degrees north of the equator off the mouth of the Orinoco River. Its total land area is only 1, 267, 650. 61 acres but don't fool yourself that that mean plenty more than a few acres a person. Most of it ain't fertile and almost half is forest. Is only about 300,000 acres what good for growing anything, but just because the population is only about 350, 000 you still can't fool yourself that is about one acre a person. If was a progressive country we did living in we woulda do everything in we power to reserve that for food, but all of it belong to the sugar and cocoa plantation owners and it in service for exportation. Nobody can't hope to touch that."

My brain like it went into the same gear it used to go in when we was in school and we had to remember what Teacher say otherwise we woulda get licks. Was the first time that happen with he, but it wasn't the last. From the time Ganesh start talking so, I used to feel like my ears raising up like a dog to listen carefully, so that I go remember what he say afterwards. Was a different kinda listening than the kind I used to enjoy with Baba. That day after Ganesh done make he proclamation, he turn he nose up and he mouth down and stop for a minute and then he say, "Well it look like this place is one that ain't arable. Although, mind you, it good for cane which can yield well on highly eluviated clays which is why you only seeing cane right around here." Then he watch me straight in my face with he blazing eye and say, "You know what your problem is, Leela. Santosh na ba, like Bap used to say. And if you don't have santosh in your heart, well, you going to keep trying to make something happen where nothing is possible." And with that he never come outside one time self to try to help me to make anything grow and I never understand what he was trying to tell me about santosh. He sure never once show me that he have any respect for anything what I was trying to do in them early days, you know.

So when I couldn't get no flowers to grow, I had to make myself content with cleaning up Ganesh books instead, and arranging them so that they woulda look as pretty as the flowers that I woulda offer if I did have any. Even in the early days I did have fifteen hundred books to play with and that was mostly what he inherit from Baba. It was all I coulda ever do with what was now Ganesh books, because plenty a the books was in Sanskrit or Hindi, and he wasn't nothing like he father. He never used to want to talk about what he read and even when I sit down right there next to him whole time, he never once turn to me and say something self like, "You know girl. This is a real nice book. Is about a cat and a dog what become friends."

The only kinda things he used to say to me was like, "Are suno, you go hot the water for me to bathe nah, girl." Or "You go bring me breakfast for me nah." Not once self he ever tell me about what he reading, even though I try to show him that that is what people should do by telling him what I read in the old *Trinidad Sentinel* or in the *Guardian* what he used to bring home from Beharry shop. Was a good thing that I used to just enjoy sitting down close by him and watching him while he read.

Aside from trying to get plants to grow, one a the first other thing I do was to put up all the holy pictures and murtis that people give we for wedding gift. Everything else Pa keep, but the kitchen wares and the holy things he give to me. Like any good dulahin, I do what Fyzabad Phua tell me and the first one I hang up in front the door was one a Ganesh Bhagwan. This was just so that me and Ganesh would always remember that he did name after the mover a all obstacles and he shouldn't worry if from time to time the almighty Ganesh move one or two *in* we way to prepare we for bigger things. Hanuman Baba was there for we protection, Vishnu Bhagwan for all blessing, Lakhshmi Mata for prosperity, and Nav Durga Mata for total coveration, a lingam to remind we a the shape and start of creation. All the other such things I put nicely in that place to make it home. Later, it was them same pictures and murtis that help to give Ganesh the reputation he develop in everybody eyes, although he add others that we didn't come with, so that everybody who come woulda feel welcome.

When no plants wouldn't come, we had to settle for buying most a we food from the dry goods side a Beharry shop and from a man who used to pass from house to house right through the village with all kinda things on a cart. He used to shout from far, "I am here. I am here." And then finally you see him. He used to have dry coconut in he cart and all, and one day, just so, when I had a few extra cents in my pocket what Pa did give me, I start to buy coconut.

Pa used to visit me often to see how I doing and every time he come he used to put one or two shilling in my hand before he leave, besides the bag a grocery and market things he used to bring with him. I can't remember which district the cartman used to get he coconut from, if is Cedros Coconut District or Nariva-Mayaro Coconut District – Cocal coconut, nah – or North Coast Coconut District. But they was very good coconut with thick, sweet, soft, firm flesh that easy to grate.

Nobody don't talk about coconut district and thing no more, though. Until I say it just now, I can't remember when last I hear somebody say that. Must be because people shame for anybody to know they does use coconut oil. But in them days the coconut estates used to do real good business, especially the Cocal estate what have trees that nobody didn't plant. They grow there for their self. I used to get very nice coconut from "I am here" which is how I did start thinking about the cartman and as a matter a fact, is from he I learn all about the districts.

I also learn how to bust the coconuts for myself with a gilpin. Pa never used to let we touch he gilpin and them, but sometimes you does know how to do something just by watching other people doing it. And I do it real good from the first try. When I done bust it and catch the water that draining out to use in what I cooking or making to drink, I dig out the coconut meat and make coconut oil and gojia so that we would be making at least some a the food we eating for weself. Sometimes I just make plain sugar cake when I didn't want to waste the flour on gojia because was war-time ration we did living by nah, and to make sugar cake you have to dry down the coconut mixture and then drop it into small separate heaps and flatten them a little bit. Beharry agree to take some a what I making to sell in the dry goods side a he shop because I refuse to let him sell anything I make in the rum shop side. But the sale wasn't very good because everybody could make their own.

I also ask 'I am Here', whose real name was Girdharie, to bring some baby chickens next time he coming. Then, when I done grate the coconut and let it sit for the cream to come up, I used to give the strain-out coconut to the chicken instead a making sugar cake. I used to mix the khikorie, what remain in the bottom a the pot after I boil down the cream and strain out all the oil, with lime pepper sauce and that used to be the tarkarie that we used to eat with roti. That was the same thing I used to do with the gheew khikorie when I take out the sarhi that remain on top a the milk that used to remain on slow fire whole day, every day, from what we didn't drink. But the cow what Pa give we, what I did name DeviDoy, didn't start to give milk until after she first bacha and that was about two years after we come to live in Fuente Grove and exactly nine months after Girdharie ask me if I ever ask the people on the estate if they go mind if I bring Devi in the pasture where they does keep the bull. Is he self who show me how to know when she ready to go.

The gheew khikorie does taste much nicer than the coconut one, and after we start having the gheew one I stop making the coconut oil one. You know how long I eh eat gheew khikorie with hot hot sada roti after you add just a little bit a salt and some lime pepper sauce to it? I dribbling just to remember. I used to make dahee with the milk remaining in the pot and every few days I used to mathé the sarhi, wash it, take out the makhan that come up and boil it down to make gheew. You could never get out all the gheew from the khikorie what remain in the bottom a the pot and I always used to like that plenty, even when I did still home by Pa and we used to get a little bit now and then from Shamoon wife, Mary, who used to mind Pa cows for we. I did like that much more than the sweet peynoose she used to bring when the cows make young one.

While I taking out the sarhi which you does always have to do patiently and carefully, I used to sing:

Dhana bhagya hamari
Dhana bhagya hamari
Krishena aiye sasurari thi

Dhana bhagya hamari
Dhana bhagya hamari
Krishena aiye sasurari thi

Maitoe kahawe ke gwalin
Maitoe kahawe ke gwalin
Kahawe ke gwalin
Kahawe me bayche dahee re dahee
Raho ghayro ley kanhaiya
Raho ghayro ley kanhaiya
Dayday ho dan dahee re dahee

Dhana bhagya hamari
Dhana bhagya hamari
Krishena aiye sasurari thi

Gokul kay gujariya
Gokul kay gujariya
Mathura may bayche dahee re dahee
Raho ghayro ley kanhaiya
Raho ghayro ley kanhaiya
Dayday ho dan dahee re dahee

Kahawe ke gwalin
Kahawe ke gwalin
Kahawe me bayche dahee re dahee
Raho ghayro ley kanhaiya
Gokula kay gujariya
Gokula kay gujariya
Mathura may bayche dahee re dahee
Raho ghayro ley kanhaiya
Raho ghayro ley kanhaiya
Dayday ho dan dahee re dahee

Suno Krishena kanhaiya
Suno Krishena kanhaiya
Lay sab bat dahee re dahee
Lay sab bat dahee re dahee
Kahar bahina Subhadra

Kahar bahina Subhadra
Arjun sang gayi re gayi
Arjun sang gayi re gayi

Kahawe ke gwalin
Kahawe ke gwalin
Kahawe me bayche dahee re dahee
Raho ghayro ley kanhaiya
Raho ghayro ley kanhaiya

Suno Krishena kanhaiya
Suno Krishena kanhaiya
Lay sab bat dahee re dahee
Kahar bahina Subhadra
Kahar bahina Subhadra
Arjun sang gayi re gayi
Suno Krishena kanhaiya

Raho ghayro ley kanhaiya
Raho ghayro ley kanhaiya
Dayday ho dan dahee re dahee
Raho ghayro ley kanhaiya

Kahar phua Kunti
Kahar phua Kunti
Bin byahe putra rahee re rahee
Kahar phua Kunti
Bin byahe putra rahee re rahee

Kahawe ke gwalin
Kahawe ke gwalin
Kahawe me bayche dahee re dahee
Raho ghayro ley kanhaiya
Raho ghayro ley kanhaiya

Dhana bhagya hamari
Dhana bhagya hamari
Krishena aiye sasurari thi

Dhana bhagya hamari
Dhana bhagya hamari
Krishena aiye sasurari thi

Hmmm. You really making me think about things I ain't think about in a long long time, you hear. But you could see from all a that, that life wasn't so bad. Things did fall into a nice repeating pattern, and after a while it was good to wake up every morning in this new place. The hardest part was probably to keep the fire going in the chulha. Four Ways did still have some forest land between the estate and the village and nobody didn't used to stop you from picking up wood from the tame-down forest that they did preserve inside the estate compound, and it had plenty trees on Baba and he brothers' land and nobody never stop you from picking up none there neither. But the Coeur de Jardin Estate was one a the older estate in the island and they didn't clean down the land and cut down every living thing to plant cane like how they did do there in Fuente Grove, which was one a the newer estate build for machines to work.

So when using the dry leaf to help make the plants grow wasn't working, I use the leaf to help to start the fire, with all the dry branch from the tree, all the coconut husk and the dry gobar what I used to collect from DeviDoy for fire too. Mostly I used to save the dry gobar for havan fire, but when I couldn't help it I use it in the cooking fire too. But I still have to walk far all about looking for wood until Girdharie start to sell wood and coals and all. I feel like he did do that especially to help me out, because one time he tell me how he had to find out where they burning coal pit and how he did start to go quite there to get the coals and wood to bring on he cart to sell. If I remembering correct, I think it was quite up Gran Couva he had to go. Yes, is Gran Couva self because he tell me how when they done take out the coals from the pit, the coalpit men does throw bhaji seed in the pit and that is where he start to get the nicest chowrai and pakchoy bhaji from, to sell.

While all this happening, the chickens getting fat on the coconut and in no time, they start to lay. When we start to get eggs from them, I make egg and orange juice for Ganesh to drink so that he would be healthy and strong. But even then, when I had chicken and cow manure and I try to make things grow, like the land get so hard, nothing coulda get through to fertilise it and it remain pack down, refusing to take in or give off any life. But arable-farable or whatever, I make we food and clothes out of what was at hand in that place because it didn't have no paradise waiting to receive we.

So that is how my life was when we start to settle down in Fuente Grove. From morning to night I working. Before morning clear, I milking DeviDoy. She was a very good girl who never give me no trouble at all. In fact, even now when I remember she I does feel to cry because I remember how when I go to she first thing in the morning, she used to kiss me and I used to start my day feeling like if she did give me a blessing. She was white with a few different shade a brown splash here and there and she had big beautiful eyes like Krishen Bhagwan eyes with long straight black eyelashes. So beautiful my girl was.

We give she and the whole set a bachiya that she give we during we Fuente Grove years to Beharry and Bhowji when we did leave, and I don't know what become a them after that. I never ask because it wasn't only we life what change after we leave Fuente Grove; Beharry and Bhowji and they children change even more. And too besides, sometimes when you done with something or you just move away from something, is not a good idea to turn around and look back. You might never recover if you do that. You might turn douen and stop just so.

But as I was saying, my morning always start with DeviDoy. When I done milk Devi, I cleaning out the cow shed and tying she out where ever I could find a place for she to graze closer to the cane fields where there was some grass and where it not going to get too hot. Lunch time I going to show she some water and change the picket spot from one place to another, and before sunset I bringing she home. Most days I used to give she the ollycake what I used to have to buy from the estate, because it good for she nah, and it keep she healthy and strong even when the grass not so good.

When I come back home in the morning from tying out the cow, if I have to bring water from the well I used to do that. But whether I getting it from the rainwater in the barrel or I bringing it from the well, first thing I used to do is full up the bath pan and heat some water for Ganesh to bathe and call him when it ready. Then I used to clean up the yard and check to see how the chickens doing, give them clean water and food and collect the eggs.

After all a that, I use to bathe and make breakfast for Ganesh because by that time he done bathe and do puja and he ready for he breakfast before he start the rest of he day around ten o' clock. As soon as he go he way, I used to do my coconut project or other projects, make lunch and change where Devi was. When I come back I give Ganesh he food and clean out the kitchen and the rest a the house, wash and iron the clothes, clean out the yard, see about the few plants and prepare food for the evening.

I did have some evening-time projects, too. I did notice, since before we marrid, that Ganesh did like a kacha taste in he food, so I used to spend plenty a my time making mango and amrak achar, and chalta, pomme cythere and tamarind kucheela and chutney and all them kinda thing. Pa used to make sure and bring some a them fruits for me whenever they in season. It used to take plenty time to do them thing because I had to grind everything on the sil and lorha. When I done do all that, then I used to go back for the cow and come home. Then I used to bathe, cook what I prepare from before and serve we the food. We eat and talk a little bit about what happening and then we get ready to sleep.

Learning to make we clothes was another adventure I should tell you about, because I know is the adventures a my life you sitting down there waiting to hear, and if you find anything I telling you fit that bill, then I can't leave out how I went back to school. Sewing did soon become a very good addition in my days. It happen so that sometimes I used to have to go very far to find a good place to tie out DeviDoy and one time I start to walk up North Trace, which was more than two miles from we house, and I realise that it had another little set a houses there just like by we. First day I went there, I pass all the house and find a good place to tie Devi.

While I walking back, I see a lady sit down in she gallery and it have some pretty pretty dress line up on racks behind she. I look up at she and smile and she raise she hand, smile back and say morning. I tell she how I admiring the dresses I seeing and she say, "Well come and have a closer look, man."

When I walk up the steps to the gallery, I see that she sitting down behind a machine sewing a dress and she have plenty more cloth spread out and done cut on a table next to she. I say, "Oh! You is a seamstress, man!" And she say, "Like you new around here or what? Everybody know me. I is Miss Mildred and everybody who is anybody in these parts know me and my family. My mammy and my granny was seamstress around here before me and I take over from where they leave off. I is really Mrs. Mildred Martin and my husband is Thomas Martin, but he ain't home right now. Both of we does sew but he alone does deliver to some a we special customers. You could just call me Miss Mildred though. That is what everybody does say."

I tell she who I is, where I living and where I come from, how I used to learn to sew and embroider in the CM school and how I did like it, and wish I coulda do it again. She say, "Well you looking like a very good girl. A seamstress work is never done and if you want to come and help me out, then I could teach you to sew."

I didn't know if Ganesh would agree with this and I tell she so. She say, "Well, you not bound to tell him. Ent I just see you walking up the road with a cow and ent you will have to come back for she? Well, if you walk a little faster while you going and coming, you could spend a hour each way with me every day and I will teach you to sew." When I went home and tell Ganesh about it, he didn't have no objections to me learning to sew, either when I was going or coming. He even say that I didn't have to worry about coming back in time to hot the water and full up the bath pan for him to bathe because he could do that for he self. So learning to sew after I tie out the cow and before I bring she back home become part a my everyday duties and help to make Ganesh take over one or two that he could do for he self.

The night-time did settle into a nice pattern too. Sometimes Ganesh used to come in my room and I used to welcome him. That was how he did arrange things from the first first night when we reach there in Fuente Grove. I remember how he did happy to see two bedrooms in the house and how straight away he say in a contented kinda voice, "You go take the back one, nah, and I going to take the front one." And from then on he used to come in my room sometimes just like he do on that first night.

I was a little frighten that first time, even though Soomintra Didi tell me not to be coward and frighten and she explain what to do. Because I was frighten when he come and stand up close in front a me with just he towel wrap around he hip that first night, I put out my hand and press it against he chest to stop him from coming too close, and I find I like how he skin feeling under my palms – smooth and soft and damp. So I let him pull me closer and I like how it feel against my face and I like how he smell like soap and the rest just fall in natural just like how Soomintra Didi did say it woulda happen. She say, "You just have to stay quiet and let him do what he want." And I do that.

I used to like it very much after that, whenever he come by me with he skin and hair damp from bathing. That first day and every day after that I used to like how he smelling nice and how he skin feeling so soft and cool and good. Sometimes he fall asleep right after and he used to remain right there whole night and I used to like that too, but he didn't do that too often. Sometimes, even when he fall asleep, he used to wake up and leave and go back in he room, but I often didn't know when that happen otherwise I mighta try to stop him.

While I moving around whole day doing things, Ganesh used to either go by Beharry shop or Beharry used to leave Bhowji in the dry goods side and the biggest boy, Suruj, in the rum shop side and come over by we. Them place was the first one you used to meet when you driving in to Fuente Grove and Ganesh did walk up back by them when he was looking around the place the next day after we come. Beharry and Ganesh become friends right away. But I didn't like them as soon as I meet them. Them kinda feelings come long after.

I remember how first first I used to get so irritated seeing Beharry coming up the walkway, eh. Whenever Beharry stand up or walking and he have nothing in he hands, he used to stick them under he shirt and rub he little round belly. Was a very bad habit. Some men does put their hand in their pocket and at least that does look decent, but anybody coulda see how Beharry hand steady moving under he shirt and sometimes it used to just stop and you used to just see one finger moving up and down, up and down.

And then he had a way of saying, for no good reason as far as I coulda see, "People can't fool me. Tom is a country-bookie but Tom ain't a fool." I sure Beharry was just playing parrot for somebody, and I don't know if is that or what, but my blood never take Beharry in them early days. It coulda be the type a shop Beharry had that make me not like him. It was selling the same thing like Pa shop, but the way Beharry make section and thing for he different goods and separate the shop in two and put bench and table for people to siddown make me think that he like to show off. Long after, I realise that is so he and Bhowji is. They just like to organise things.

But I think the thing that used to bother me most of all is the fact that after that first day, when I didn't pay much mind, because it was part a Ganesh telling me what he see when he went for he walk, every day after that is either I had to see Beharry or I had to hear about him. Because in all the years, although Ganesh never tell me what he read, he coulda never done tell me all what Beharry say. That is all the two of them used to do whole day, just siddown there, labar-labar, bakar-bakar. And clearly most a the talk had to do with how wise and knowledgeful Ganesh was and how glad Beharry is that Ganesh come Fuente Grove to live because finally he going to have some intelligent company. And Ganesh didn't like nothing so much as to keep repeating the good things Beharry say to him about him.

And then one day, good or bad, the routine I did set up for my Fuente Grove days suddenly shatter after nearly five years a building it piece by careful piece. I can't remember who come to visit we that day, but I remember saying, "That is all he good for. You know how much I does tell him not to read all the time. But you can't stop him from reading. Night and day he reading." Well that night, the door for my room open and I expecting Ganesh to walk into the room just like he always used to do when he ready, so I turn over to face him with a smile just as I always used to do. But Ganesh didn't come right in like he accustomed to and he looking just like he look whole day. He just stand up in the

59

doorway not moving and that is when I notice he have a belt wrap around he knuckles with the end hanging down. I sit up one time and roll off the bed and watch he in he face. He wasn't looking vexed but he start coming towards me and he saying as he coming, "Girl, you make me shame today. You disrespect me today. You treat me like I ain't worth nothing."

By that time, he close enough to me and he raise he hand and start to bring it down so that he could make the belt wrap around my shoulder and fall on my back. Same time he saying, "You have to promise never to do it again." I rush at him and grab the belt one time before he could bring it down full and I say, "I promise. I promise. I promise." And with my next hand I push him on the chest, one time, two time, and push him back through the door. He stumble when I make the last hard push and I let go the belt same time and he fall. I close the door and lock it behind him. He start to pound on the door, shouting, "Leela. Leela. Open this door, girl. I is you husband. You can't lock me outta any room in my own house."

I ain't say nothing. I sit down on my bed and watch the door for a long while and stop listening to anything he saying and when I realise that the place quiet quiet and he give up on he vengeance, I lie down and think that I shoulda know better. The way Ganesh did start enjoying what Beharry saying about him and how much book he read and all that kinda thing shoulda warn me that I better start to talk good about Ganesh and he reading, too. He used to buy book every time he go San Fernando and, from after that, I start to talk up about how much new inch a book he buy. Every time he put on them brown shoes and brown hat, blue shirt and khaki pants and take up Baba walking stick to go San Fernando to see he lawyers what say they fighting the case against Kaka claim, I know he coming back with one or two new book to add to the pile that he and Beharry getting free by post from all the coupons they fulling out and sending. And so I start to talk highly about every inch he read and the few inches he manage to write. But not from the very next day.

That night I couldn't sleep. I just lie down there thinking that I not letting nobody try to hit me after all what I put into making we life together, and when the four o'clock cock start crowing I get up and pack a bag with a few things. I write a note for Ganesh to read when he get up, and I went back, although not in the same way we come, to Four Ways. That was Girdharie cart day and I walk round to the top a the road leading into the estate because he used to go there first, and from the time he come, I tell him that I waiting for him because I have to go back Four Ways and I don't know how to do it by myself. Girdharie tell me climb up in the cart. He ain't even stop to sell one thing self and he carry me straight home.

My father hug me up tight when I reach and like he did done start to cry from the time he spot me with my one bag coming home alone against the hard mid-morning light. Because when my face rest against he own, it was wet and I feel it was with tears. But all he say is, "Bayti, you alright?" And I say, "Yes, Pa. But I tired, so I just come home to stay with you for a little bit." He say, "Go go. Put away your bag and change your clothes and thing. You always welcome to stay in your father house for as long as you please." And then he tickle me under my chin like he used to do when we was little girls and when I smile, he turn me around and push me inside with he palm flat between my shoulders.

CHAPTER 4: MR STEWART AND ME: THE BIGGEST TURNING POINT

I did wonder if I make a big mistake to come back to Fourways until Mr Stewart come on the scene. It was Soomintra Didi who did make me feel bad. She hardly come to visit Pa, but when she hear I leave Ganesh and come back by Pa, she start to come regular to hurt my head with she old talk and showing off.

First, I see how she did start to dress up like she is Saudamini in *Amar Jyoti*. I never see that show. Is she self who say, "I feels like I is Saudamini." From the time Ranjit Kumar bring the first Indian film come to Trinidad and Tobago in 1935 – *Bala Joban* was the name of that one – Soomintra Didi going cinema. But I never did get to go to them in them early days and it was plenty more years before I know what she mean and what going to the cinema was like. It don't have the same effect on everybody but it was one a the thing that did start to make Soomintra Didi behave the way she does still behave. First time I just thinking, well it look like this Saudamini ain't a nice person at all. Because I can't begin to describe for you how Soomintra Didi start to carry on as though she come from somewhere else. She start to talk in a way I never hear nobody else talk – well, like some of them who turn CM Christians. And most a she talk was just schupid talk about how she children, Jawaharlal and Sarojini, and the ones still to come, Motilal and Kamala, and she and she husband doing this and liking that.

Later, after the war, she used to talk non-stop about how they went on this holiday and that holiday, in which plane, which boat and what ship and what hotel them stay in, and what they eat and what they wear and Pa listen and beam and smile as though she saying that she went Bhagvat Yagya and make plenty sacrifice or something. What I come to believe is that long before Soomintra

Didi wanted to be Saudamini, she did get to be like all the CM people we did know from school and when them start to behave like Saudamini, she just follow suit. Was so since Soomintra Didi thought she woulda get pick to be monitor and she start going to church every Sunday morning. Thank God she never keep up the habit, and never dress up them poor children and carry them go to church every Sunday or to help out in church bazaar and thing just to show off. But that is probably only because she was never too much into the helping thing, and if you going to church, they expect you to help and to take the cyatechism to everybody.

But I never had no doubt, especially after I get to know more a that kinda high falutin people in San Fernando and Port of Spain, that she behaviour was exactly the same as them one, and like all a them, when Indian independence time come, all of a sudden she did start to dress up in sari to go all about. As a matter a fact, although I does still say Didi, you wouldn't believe how much time she buff me and tell me not to call she that after she get marrid and went San Fernando to live with she husband, who care about nothing in this world beside the things he own.

I don't understand up to now why Pa couldn't see through what Soomintra Didi doing when she raising she arms and setting them to swinging, just so she could jangle she gold bracelets for everybody to see. And is in which high society she coulda learn to cough, hawk, but not spit is beyond me. That is such a nasty thing to do. And then, just because Pa used to admire how Ganesh does read and write, she forever finding a chance to say thing like, "Jawaharlal father start reading the other day too. He always say that if he had the time he woulda do some writing, but with all the coming and going in the shop he ain't really have the time, poor man. I don't suppose Ganesh so busy, eh?" That is the kinda thing my sister start to say to me after I leave Ganesh and come back to Fourways.

Pa used to real spoil them children too when Soomintra Didi come to visit and he couldn't done giving them things and showing them off to the few fellas that used to still come and siddown in front the shop in the evening. "Come nah, Jawaharlal. Let Ramanand and them boys see how big my grandson getting and what a good-looking boy he is." And Ramanand, who always ready to be pleasant, saying, "The boy want a lollipop?" Pa couldn't stop praising Soomintra Didi and admiring the car what bringing she and the children to see him. He tell she, "You coming like royalty now. Four Ways can't handle people with your distinction." He and the driver used to examine every inch a the engine and the trunk and the upholstery and even the door hinge and the windshield wiper and they used to talk about it like if is them self what build the car. All a that used to make me feel so sad.

But the whole thing change one day when Soomintra Didi and she band a children get into their car and leave. The driver hold the door open for all a them to get in while I watching the ground and seeing how Soomintra Didi shoe-heel leaving holes in the pitch what Pa get spread right around the shop, and she turn round by the car door with one foot inside and she still talking, talking and then finally she get in and they pull off in a cloud a dust as soon as the car hit the road. Pa turn around now from waving at them, with a broad smile on he face, and he say how he going by Chinta Mausi because he ain't see she in so long. He even tell me to run in the shop quick and put a few things in a bag for him to carry for she. But I know right away that he really going to show off about Soomintra Didi and how good she living and then Mausi go start to tell him about she children and how good them getting along, about which part them going and what thing them doing.

But none a them going to say a word about me because all a them sorry for me and shame a little bit about how me and Ganesh get throw outta we own house before I could even start to be a wife, and how I did have to come back home after just a few years, and how I in Four Ways for so long now and Ganesh never come to see me self. And is not as if is a strange thing. Plenty other woman leave and come back home and is not as though I marrid to a man who is a thief or a gaol-bud or some kind a disgrace like that, or anything. But I know that that is how it will be in everybody mind and it didn't have nothing I coulda do about it. I did know exactly how Pa and Chinta Mausi going to pretend I don't exist, just like plenty people, who used to talk to me normal normal before I get marrid, does try not to ask me for nothing when they come in the shop these days. Is time to go back to

Fuente Grove, I was thinking, even though Ganesh never ask me to come back, because I was feeling so fed up.

It was me one alone in the shop after Pa leave. I did siddown crying on a bench in the corner right inside the door and I didn't hear anybody come in. I didn't even realise anybody was there until this man all a we know as Mr Stewart come right right up to me where I did khukray in the corner and he say, "I never expected to see the wife of blessed Ganesh, daughter of lucky Ramlogan and chosen daughter of Pandit Ramsumair sitting in a corner and crying so sadly all by herself." He kneel down in front a me to bring he face in line with mine and then he put he big hands on my shoulders and before I know what is what, my head fit up under he chin and my face bury in he orange clothes. I will never forget how he smell, not in this janam or any other. It was like nothing I did ever smell before. Not totally like a ram goat but very close to it. The smell make me kinda gag for breath and I raise my head up to breathe in properly and it stop my tears one time.

When we was still living in Fourways, Ganesh tell me how he meet this Mr Stewart, a whiteman from Scotland who plenty a the villagers was calling a madman, but Ganesh say he feel he wasn't mad at all. He was just a seeker of wisdom.

I think he sense when my attention shift from my own troubles and turn to him completely, and he bring one a he hand around from where he did wrap them around my back and he turn up my face. My orhni slide off my hair when he do that, and that, as they say, was the beginning a that. Every day after that Stewart coming in the shop now, sometimes in the middle a the day when it quiet, and he finding one thing or another to tell Pa that he must go and check out, as far from the shop as he could make him go. I used to just pull my orhni over my mouth so Pa wouldn't see that I laughing. Over the next few weeks, I feel like Stewart spend all he time watching the shop door when he not inside the shop just talking and reading the papers for Pa, and once he get Pa to leave he used to come to be with me and we used to close the shop door behind Pa and the world used to disappear.

We get a little more brave after about the first two weeks and instead a just staying together in the house after we find a way to get Pa to leave, sometimes I used to go and meet Stewart instead.

The first first time we meet outside was under the samaan tree in the middle a where they make the golf course on the estate now, and that same day, because he say I did done come so far already, he say he want me to see the house he living in on the other side a the estate. So we start to meet there sometimes. But we favourite place to meet end up being right here on this property, because outta all the places I get to know in my life, it will always be the place I love the best because it was Baba own and the only place that I roam freely without a care.

One day I was telling Stewart that, before we get to know one another, I woulda never imagine we could be so alike, because like him, I used to roam all over this place by myself when I was a little girl. He grab me tight and tell me that he don't want me doing that now that I is a big girl. I keep my mouth shut about the fact that I used to do that in Fuente Grove when I was looking for water seep in the ground and almost every day I used to do it when I going with my cow and she bachiya in front or behind me.

I woulda probably say something about Fuente Grove, but then he ask me where I used to go when I was little and he was sounding worried. So I start to tell him quick that I was always safe when I was a little girl because the only place I used to walk about was on this property belonging to Baba and he brother and sister. I never went nowhere near the boundary where the oil derricks was, and where it always have people because a that. I used to walk about only inside the boundary line that Baba did plant around they land to block it off from the pieces they give up for the oil company to do their drilling and extracting. So then Stewart ask me if I woulda mind showing him where I used to go walking about.

I did know everything about this place and I did tell Stewart everything I know. I tell him how Baba piece was nine acres, Dada piece was ten, Kaka piece was ten and Phua piece was five and we walk over the whole thing except for round Kaka piece. I explain how Babu buy it so from different owners over the years because he and he brothers, and none a the other people in Four Ways as a matter of fact, didn't inherit nothing from the land settlement scheme. Pa say he remember how he grandfather say he cry when they tell him he didn't have no proof that he father is he father and the five acres they was living and planting on was now the state property after he grandfather dead. He say that is how he father had to go back to work on the estate. Because he couldn't bear to go back on the one where he did born and that is why he move up to the Coeur de Jardin.

I tell Stewart how Baba used to cultivate all the pieces besides Kaka piece and that Ganesh own all now apart from Kaka one, and he also inherit the hundred acres in Fyzabad what did belong to Phua from she husband side. After Ganesh leave for England, I used to be worried that I would have to see about inheritance before I dead unless Ganesh come back and attend to he own business for a change. I used to think that it would be only right if I leave it for the children what Babu brothers did have and I used to worry that I don't know them and I don't even know if they still in Trinidad and Tobago and I would have to go around enquiring about them. But hahaha, what wrong with me today. We not talking about that right now either.

We talking about how I introduce Stewart to where I used to roam. I don't have to describe it for you. You seeing how Baba cultivate this place with your own eyes. I didn't change nothing since I come back. Once a week, I have some a the fellas in the village, what I know from long time, coming to clean up the place and take off the bird vine and cut off cheepo from the citrus trees and thing, but I never do nothing much more than that kinda maintenance. All a this is Baba work and he make it like Vrindavan in truth, eh?

What I like best about it is how you does feel like you walking about in a wild place that was here forever, except that if you know anything about anything, you will know that is not possible. When you was driving in from the gate self, you probably notice that as far as you eye could see, it have parrot heliconia, ground orchid and white stamp and red fern growing on the ground. That woulda never happen if it didn't have cashew trees plant here before. You see, once upon a time, it did have big big cashew growing for export project in Trinidad and Babu did take part in that. When some people talking about him, some does still say the Cashew Nut King. That time, almost the whole hundred acres belonging to Babu and he two brothers was in cashew, and for some reason both parrot heliconia and ground orchid like under the cashew trees and now, when the trees get old, it look like lycopodium love growing from the branches a the trees and ground fern like it below.

Baba chop down plenty cashew for other plants afterwards, and we don't really gather the nuts from the few trees no more except when them boys in the village feel to roast some just for their own self, and then they does clean them and bring some for me too. But the heliconia and ground orchid still growing strong and almost for the whole year it does have flowers. Baba was the one who clear the cashew to plant the other trees and plenty kinda flowers that he say it important to cultivate. He plant bargad, anjeer, neem, jamun, plenty plenty different kinda mango and zaboca, a few sapodilla, some mamisipote, some star-apple, some pomme cythere, tamarind, and chinee tamarind, some sour cherry, some carambola, a few amrak and chalta, one or two breadfruit, katahar and chataigne and plenty citrus and a good bit a cocoa and coffee what he did get for free from the extension services. When the government was promoting the citrus cultivation and he went to get plants, he did get the cocoa and coffee too.

The bargad and anjeer plant mainly where Baba did turn two piece into pasture for the cows. It don't have no cows no more though. Ganesh did tell Pa to sell all what it had when we had to leave because a Kaka, and he did add that money to the tin we did full the kitcheree money in, which was all that we did have to start up we life in Fuente Grove. If you take a walk that side you will see how big the bargad and anjeer come and because the pasture was fertilise good with the cow manure, the tannia, dasheen and yam them fellas does plant still growing there good. I feel that is because the pasture did come like everybody property over the years, and every year when somebody reaping they does chook back the head for the next year. When you walking so, you will also see that Baba plant a good few chenette, caimite and pommerac trees too, and them get real big now and even the few fat pork and cerise bush does look like trees. You will see plenty more when you take the walk around you say you have to make, to see with your own eye what I talking about.

Baba plant everything in such a way that it come like circles inside circles, next to circles, right through the whole property. The trees did form a circle around the house and the kutya, and between the circle a trees and the buildings, like I say, he plant up plenty plenty different kinda flowers – urahu and all kinda other normal hibiscus, chameli, ixora, plenty frangipani and allamanda and a good few tuberose, marigold, rose, zinnia, lady slippers, old maid and plenty different kinda anthurium, that I promising myself to separate and spread out.

Farther away from the house, where it don't have heliconia and thing on the ground, it used to have petit tambu and pineapple. The pine does need a little bit a care because you does have to keep harvesting the fruit and replanting it, just like you does have to do with the fig, moko and plantain patch and them.

But I suppose to be telling you about Stewart and the land. When I bring him for the walk, and he see what I telling you about, he say he could see why I love the place so much. He say if he did ever have to tell anybody where to shoot the scene where Shakuntala and Dushyant meet, this would be it for sure.

While we walking through the property and I showing Stewart which trees I used to climb, which fruits I used to wait to eat, and where in the river I used to bathe, I end up telling him almost my whole life story. I tell him how sad I was when we did first come here to live because a how Ma dead and how I find myself in Baba place without knowing I was here. Baba find me on top a orange tree eating portugal what I did pick while I was walking through the field, and from that first day, he welcome me into he life. When he see me eating the portugal, he say, "Hmm. Like both a we doing the same thing this morning, Radhayshyam. We making sure everything running smooth on the property. You want to come go with me to survey the rest." I like he smiley face one time and when he hold out he hand I put mine in he own and jump down from the branch.

As we walking, Baba showing me where I could go and warning me how, while they was exploring, the oil people did make deep sinks in the land that used to full up with water in the rainy season. While we going from place to place, Baba was stopping to talk to people who working on all kinda different thing. Some did building a long high house shape with bamboo, and when I ask him what it is, he tell me they making a machan for karaili and it have plenty more all over with bodi, saim, barbadine, passion fruit and thing. Was the first time I did see a whole machan build so for them thing. Most people use to just chook a single bamboo with plenty branch in the ground for the vines to run on. He show me what trees to eat from and because jamun was in season, he teach me how to know which ones ripe enough to eat. He show me how to choose cerise the same way and how to roll them between my palms to soften them before I eat them.

Then he say, "Now I going to show you a track to a place you might like." A little while after he say that, we come just so to the river running through the land to the northern side. He show me how I could walk from stone to stone without wetting my foot and warn me that I will never be able to do that in the rainy season because I mightn't be able to see the stones and I should never think that I could remember where they is because, in the rainy season, the river does be very deep and the current does be very strong. When we get to the other side we just had to walk up a little hill and it bring we straight to the kutya.

We walk from there and up the steps to right where we is now and Baba make me come over to this window right here and he point and say, "And that is where you living. When you going back, you could walk straight so, and if you ever want to find me, you just have to come back straight up the hill." We become friends right away and from that very first day I remember how he used to say over and over again that oil don't employ and unless we keep on planting what we going to eat, two major problems going to take we over. We going to starve and people will have no work to do.

What I telling you now is what I was telling Stewart then, and I was so happy showing him everywhere I used to go, telling him where I used to just sit down and idle and what I used to be dreaming and thinking.

But you know, I think I should explain to you that this thing between Stewart and me didn't just happen so outta the blue, when he find me crying in the shop, you know. Only thing is I didn't realise what it did mean when it first first happen. The thing start since Stewart come to Four Ways and he coming to the shop to buy one or two things from time to time. That was long before Ganesh come back home. After things happen between we, is only then I remember how from the first day he see me, I see how he couldn't stop watching me.

Sometimes he try to make conversation. But I only saying good morning or good evening or whatever, and running away because it had something about he eyes that look a little bit like Baba and Ganesh one, but more like the colour a the morning sky than like young leaves against the morning light. Something about them used to make me feel very frighten. I feel like they boring straight through me. I couldn't look back at them. And knowing that he watching me make me feel like I hearing my own heart beating and I couldn't hear anything he saying. I used to worry that he go think I gunga-sunga or something, because I used to feel like if I gone deaf and like the ground get unsteady, and I couldn't see too good because my eye used to start to run even though I know that I not crying.

Them was such strange feelings, eh, and first first I thought that maybe I was catching malkadi. But my kinda malkadi wasn't a sometime thing. It was permanent because the feelings never go away, you know. Even up to now, I feel if he appear right now everything will be just like it was then. Who knows? Maybe even the ears and eyes will react same way again. I never hear anybody else ever talk about anything like that happening to them, even up to now. When it start, I used to think I fraid him because he was a stranger, and that is why them things was happening. I didn't know it was something else until them same eye turn into the doorway I used to walk through to enter we own place in creation.

When he and Ganesh start meeting and talking after Baba dead and we was going to get marrid, sometimes they used to siddown right there in the shop and I used to feel him watching me every time I passing. Hahaha. Yes is just so. "*Everytime I pass, you look at me.*" But it would a have to be: "*I go tell me father not to send me down there.*" After this thing happen with we, then I start thinking that he did probably make friend with Ganesh just because he hear everybody in the village starting to talk about how me and Ganesh going to get marrid. But in them days I try not to come nowhere

71

near to where he is, because from the time he reach close to me, or if I even hear he voice, I feel like something happen inside a my head and inside my belly. And sometimes the pain in my stomach used to be so bad I used to think I would vomit right there in front a him.

So maybe this thing that come and happen between we was always waiting to happen. And you know, sometimes it does still make me feel confused that the way I did feel when we first meet, like I hearing my heart beating and all a that, that them feelings never went away in all the days I know him. When I talking about him even right now, I feeling so a little bit still. I used to feel like I going to choke with excitement and that was a part of how I feel every minute a every hour that we spend together. Full up. I think that might be the best way to explain how I used to feel – full up and overflowing.

A, A! But look at my crosses! I never expect nobody to ask me such a question in my life. Is me who cause you to ask if I would mind elaborating on my sex life, ent? What kinda question is that? Is my fault for starting up the talk in the first place about mine and Stewart business, ent? Oh lord, oy. That was the very thing I thought mightn't have to come up in this storytelling, oui. My sex life! I never think about it so and as a matter a fact, I prefer how some people does say making love, because I think that that does describe what does happen better. But no, for your information, I not shame to talk about anything because I ain't have no regrets about nothing I ever do in my whole life. A person life is their life and that is all it have to it. It is what it is because of what that person do in their many other lives and whether you like it or not it will affect the many more lives the person have to live. Nothing to shame or regret in that. As I saying, it is what it is.

And, you know, it might be a good thing to talk about what you asking me and it might be a good subject for we institute here to pick up, because the few years I live in town teach me very well how people does look at people they thinking of as Indian woman – which is how you and all call me first first. Like they does think we as oversexed. Maybe we is. I don't know. I don't even care to know. Because I wouldn't change nothing that happen to me, or what I do, is a better way to put it, in that department. I must tell Mildred and the rest a the group that we must find a way to open up the talk in the institute on that subject.

I mean, even now as we talking, I remember how I did come to want and wait for when he woulda walk up behind me quiet quiet on he big bony bare white foot and wrap he hands around me to pull me back against him. If I didn't see with my own eyes that sometimes he coulda become soft, I woulda think that the man was always hard because a that memory. If that is what oversexed mean, then I is a real Indian woman for true. But the way I look at it, he was a piece a my good luck in this life and I only feel great thankfulness for everything we did have together.

I remember how when he stand up behind me with he arms wrap around me from behind, like so, I used to feel as if nothing couldn't a reach inside a that circle to touch me, far less to hurt me. It was like a sacred place. I used to feel as if I protected from all the evils a the world when he do that. I used to feel I just want to stay there forever. But then, from the time he shift the slightest littlest bit from that position, I used to adjust and wait for more. By the time he start to run he palms down over my hip bones with all he fingers kinda massaging soft and gentle, I used to become something else, a different half-unconscious me.

I remember how he hands used to move from hip to belly and then when they press down a little harder just below my navel, my head used to fall back against he chest. And when he mouth come down on my forehead, then my eyes used to close and I used to have to try to just keep breathing and wait for the rest to happen to finish me off again and again and again. Because now that I thinking about it, it was a general kinda pattern he used to follow. While he mouth used to prevent me from thinking because a its movement on my hair, my forehead, my neck or my cheeks, he used to start to gather up my skirt slow slow, although he keeping me all this time standing up and press-up hard from top to bottom against he whole body.

I remember how I used to feel the breeze on my shin bone and then my knees and then my legs as though the breeze and all helping him to keep me in that state. And then I used to feel he hand against bare skin and by that time I couldn't a do nothing to prevent sound from coming outta my mouth. And is then he used to stick he thumb inside me, just like how a child does stick she thumb inside she mouth, and I never ask him, but I used to feel that I behaving just like the child mouth on the child thumb. He used to make me feel like I exploding with that finger first and then he used to turn me around and start all over with he mouth from the top of my head down down down, not leaving out a spot until he reach where he hands and thumb just leave. I still don't know how and when he used to take off my clothes or what he used to do with he own, which wasn't never much in any case. Most days was just the ugly orange gown that he did think make him the wali he profess to be or maybe the bhaklol sadhu I hear Ganesh call him sometimes. Other days it used to just be khaki short pants and white short sleeve shirt and nothing else.

I remember the way he fingers used to move on my legs and back and arms, so soft that it was almost as though is the air what moving. That used to cause every hair on my head and body to stand up on end by the time he stand up face to face with me again – or face to chest because I used to have to tilt my head back to be face to face. It had something about the way he used to use his fingers on my body, as though he don't really want to disturb me, that used to have the exact opposite effect. And I telling you, I will never ever forget he mouth, just like I will know them fingers anywhere in any janam. From day one, it was like I did always know that mouth, always so soft but same time always so strong, hard almost – on my eye, my mouth, my ribs, my nipples, my hipbone, my belly, my navel and by the time it reach where he thumb did like to be, I never coulda think at all, and I didn't care if people condemn me and I never went to nobody heaven.

Only when I get so – and I can't figure out up to now how he used to know when the time was just right for him to take it to a next level – then he used to pick me up and when my legs wrap around him, then he used to siddown and slide me down on top a him, and I think I used to dead a little bit every single time and he alone used to be the centre that my life start to revolve on, instead a flying right outta my body like it was trying to do. I think that is how things remain between we up to now, like two vines stretching for each other against the pull a we own roots, taking strength only from the way we knot up together. In them days, it was like the reaching used to take us to we own personal heaven, and I never wanted then or now to be in any other people one. I didn't care about anything else then, at all at all. I didn't care for anything but knowing that he was there in the world and wanted me, only me, just like how he wanted me like that, every day, many many times for the day.

And let me tell you something, what start to make me feel even more excited and happy in later days was when I realise that when I touching him, he used to feel just like how I used to feel when he touching me. One time I just rest my hand on he bare chest unexpectedly to steady myself as I was stepping outta my skirt, and he grab my hand and hold it against him and he eyes look so much like if he going to cry that I get worried one time. I drop the skirt and hold on to him with my next hand and ask him what happen. He breathe in and then he answer me with a strange kinda smile as he breathing out, "Leannan. Nothing happened. It's just that even your fingertips cause five tiny rivers of fire to travel over me from head to toe. How do you do this? What kind of power is that, mo chridhe?"

I push him away and I say, "Well is not me who have the power. Is you. Is you what doing thing to me what I didn't know nobody coulda ever do before." It was one a the only time I could remember that we ever say anything about how we feeling or what we doing and it was like a big revelation for the two a we same time, especially me. Is the strangest feeling in the world, I telling you, you know – to feel so powerless and so powerful same time – to know that somebody else life is yours to do anything you want to do with it and yours is as helpless in front a them in the same way. And the next thing is that you don't need that power for nothing, you know, and you will never use it because is really like it using you. When I know that the two a we have the same amount a power, then I start to do whatever I did feel to do with he body just like how he used to do with mine.

I never ever tell nobody about this time in my life before, you know, and me and Stewart never talk much at all about what we doing or feeling, except for what I telling you today. We used to just be together and wanted nothing else but to be, just so, forever. Most a the time, the sounds we make wasn't really about making words. They was something else, like a language between only me and he and not one that passing just between we head alone. I don't know how nobody else never realise that something big did happen to me because I was never the same after that first touch. Maybe I was never the same after he walk into the village. Who knows? But it was a bigger turning point for me than when my mother or Baba dead or when I get marrid to Ganesh or when I set up house in Fuente Grove. It was and will always be the biggest thing that ever happen to me. Maybe like all sacred things, it was so natural that nobody didn't notice, didn't know what they was seeing even though it right in front a them and they seeing it with their own two eye.

Ganesh, at least, shoulda realise that something happen, but if the thought ever cross he mind he never say a word to me. He just lie back and take in the new person who went back to Fuente Grove with he because that is what happen after Stewart disappear. When Ganesh come back for me, it was more than a year since I did leave Fuente Grove and the very next day after Stewart tell me the story about Shakuntala and Dushyant and together we plant a frangipani and a bargad tree. Sometimes, over the years, I used to stop just so in the middle a some very ordinary day and long for Ganesh to be just a little bit self like Stewart to make the emptiness that never go away feel a little better.

I was out in the back gallery standing up by the machan washing wares and dreaming about meeting Stewart later when I see Ganesh. When I tell you, I did feel to take all the dirty water and throw it down on top a he head, standing there watching up at me in he suit and hat and tie with a schupid grin on he face. I tell him, "You better move from there before I pitch this bowl a dirty water over your face and wash away that grin, you hear." He raise he hand and show me a little book he holding in it, smaller than the copy book I used to use in school. He announce that he done write he first book and then he say, "Oh, I come back for you, girl."

When he come inside the shop, just for something to do, I take the book from he: *101 Questions and Answers on the Hindu Religion*.

And when I look inside the book I see that most a the thing he write was what everybody did know already, and some a the thing he write was thing nobody, certainly not me, did ever hear before. I mean I did learn about the ten commandments in CM school, but I did never know that we had commandments too. But in that book, Ganesh write down that we have nine. I don't know what make he decide we must have one less. Up to now, I does still remember them because he make me learn them off after I settle back down in Fuente Grove. They was:

1. Thou shalt maintain fellowship with the saints.
2. Thou shalt have unceasing love for thy scriptures.
3. Thou shalt honour and serve thy guru.
4. Thou shalt sing the praises of God with steadfast devotion.
5. Thou shalt recite the name of God with unwavering faith.
6. Thou shalt practice self-control and pursue a course of conduct outlined in the holy scriptures.
7. Thou shalt recognise God in all forms of creation without any discrimination whatsoever.
8. Thou shalt practice contentment.
9. Thou shalt be honest and straight forward in all one's dealings with others.

As though he wanted to make sure people understand the commandments, he did also put a section in the book what had the headline: What are the creeds of a Sanatanist? It still have some copies of that book on the bookshelf here you know. Let me show you. You see? It seem to me that the answers was things we did know and never bother to talk about knowing. I find, though, the way how he write some a them did change the exact meaning a what we does believe in and live we life by. Look at how he write them:

1. I believe in God, the unity behind the manifold universe, the changeless truth that is behind all appearances, transcendent over all and immanent in all, the Divine Essence that permeates the Universe.
2. I believe that God assumes form from time to time as the creating, preserving power of the universe into whom it eventually returns.

3. I believe that man is not only a gross material body, nor yet a finer organ called the mind or intellect but is something greater called the Atma.

4. I believe that the Soul is a part of the Divine Essence and by nature pure and perfect, infinitely powerful and blessed, was never created, will never end and will move from body to body until it achieves perfection.

5. I believe in the laws of Karma and that I am the Creator of my own destiny, that my present condition is due to my past conduct and my future condition depends on my present conduct.

6. I believe that the Vedas, Upanishads, the Puranas, the Shastras, the Mahabharat, the Ramayan and the Bhagavad Gita contain all the truths.

That day, when he come back for me, while I looking through the book, I wondering why he did want to write it at all and why he spend so much time and waste so much energy doing it, because plenty a them things we did done know and plenty a them we didn't bound to know. I couldn't understand who he write that book for and I mighta tell him to take he schupid book and go back Fuente Grove because I was liking my life in Pa house as much as I used to like it when I used to spend time with Baba every day, but plenty plenty more now than then, although I wouldn't tell Ganesh or anybody else the reason for that part.

So I just give he back he book, and I stamp my foot and tell him no, I not going back. I say, "Eh, eh. Is more than a whole year now since you beat me and drive me from your house, and in all that time you never bother to send a message to ask, 'Dog, how you is? or, cat, how you is?'" He say, "Oh but listen to me nah, man; is you who leave me, and I couldn't a send you no message because I writing to show you that I could do what I tell your father I going to do. I working hard so." I ready to tell him then how I not going to tolerate nobody ignoring me just because they 'working hard so', because I really done make up my mind not to go back with him. I mean here in Pa house I really didn't have nothing much to do and on top a that I had Stewart and he was making me feel so happy and he was reading and writing poetry for me, which is something Ganesh never do.

But same time, all ruction break loose, the second but not the last time Ganesh cause that in my father house. Ganesh never think carefully about anything he doing, eh, and he didn't think how much people woulda get hurt when he dedicate the book to Beharry and leave all a we, who consider we self he family, outta it. Pa get so upset and start getting on so much. From the time Pa start up with, "You give that kind of a man the book rather than your own father-in-law", I did think it was best to just take Ganesh and leave Four Ways.

But as soon as I think everything cool down enough and everybody start to feel normal again, just about a month after I went back with him to Fuente Grove, I tell Ganesh I going back to see Pa because I not really happy about how we leave him feeling that day. Really and truly, though, it was to see Stewart and tell him how much I missing him and that he have to figure out a way for the two a we to be together. I did want him to know that I would go with him and be with him anywhere in the world that he want to be, even if is in that old estate house right here in Four Ways. I wanted to tell him that wherever he choose is where we going to bring up this child that was growing inside a me and the many more that we will have together.

But when I reach home, Pa say Mr Stewart come to see him the day after me and Ganesh leave. Pa say he tell Mr Stewart all what happen and he say Mr Stewart did look very sad and worried, but he still take he time and explain to Pa that he shouldn't mind too much about the dedication in the book, because a man must always be true to heself and Ganesh was expressing the truth about the book when he say it come into being only because a Beharry. Pa say, "He tell me something bout how Beharry is Ganesh buse or ruse or something so, and nobody can't tell a man who should be he ruse. I didn't understand what he mean because it sound like something you woulda say about a man wife, but I didn't question him more because I didn't want to look schupid by saying I don't know what a buse or a ruse is."

Pa say how the next week Mr Stewart come back again, looking even more maga and bony than he used to always look, and he tell Pa how everything that could go wrong going wrong in he life. He tell Pa how he get in a fight with he doctor-physician friend from Scotland name Vincent who living in St Clair, because Vincent step outta line and write in he diary about some private things what Stewart tell him, and that adding to the urgency for him to leave Trinidad, because he never wanted to offend anybody or to hurt anybody and if he karma is to walk alone, so be it. Pa say that Mr Stewart say that he want me to know that, on penalty a he life, nobody name in Four Ways will ever be called because he make holes where names should be in that diary.

Pa say that the next week Mr Stewart come back again and hand him a envelope with Leela Ramsumair write big on the front and he tell him that he finally make up he mind to go back to Scotland so that he could die in peace in the place he ancestors was forced to leave, but which it was in he power to reclaim. He beg him on pain of death not to open the envelope, that Pa had to put it directly in my hand when I alone, just as how he was putting it in Pa one. When Pa done tell me that, eh, I feel like all the sadness what make up this life a mine, like it never go end. And I did never feel like I want it to end so much as I did want it to end that day.

That is how I feel that day and many many times over the years. The sadness used to just take me over and I used to have to force myself to get up and start moving to make it go away. I don't know how to explain that sadness to you. Is like if you suck something with poison and you feel how it burning like a fire blazing and it shape like a upside-down V right here in the centre a where your ribs join above your belly. I feel so sad that I woulda never see him again, never feel him again. It take a long long time for me to accept that is so some things in life does have to be. Whether they make you happy or sad, you just have to accept them as they is and sometimes that is a very very hard kinda accepting to have to do.

When I open the envelope, my eye and Pa one nearly come outta we head. The envelope did full a money in wads mark $100, $500, $1,000, $5,000 and $10,000. All a them had a picture of a man looking like a lady on it (that is how Pa describe it). Pa take up one and then another a the different ones and he saying, "Girl, this is US dollars – not British money you know. They used to say how Mr Stewart does really give away money to people. And it look like he choose to give away this set to you before he go back where he come from." I see like a letter inside when Pa taking out the wads one by one and playing with them, and I take it quick and hide it in my bosom and I tell Pa, "Pa you know what. I think you should hold on to this for me, because what I go do with this kinda money in Fuente Grove." Before I leave to go, though, I change that a little bit to tell Pa, "Whenever you go San Fernando, if you could change it to smaller a we money and bring some for me I go be glad." Pa ain't ask no question, just as I did expect. When it come to money matters, Pa did always have he head screw on the right way on he shoulders.

I didn't know how to find Stewart, and what I thought would be a letter telling me how to do that was just he way a saying goodbye, he leaving. I went by the house where he used to stay but when I ask the one or two people I see around there, none a them didn't have no information about him. He really never tell me nothing about heself and I didn't know where to turn. I didn't know who this Vincent person was who he talk to Pa about. For days I just roaming all over the estate and all about on Baba property and walking by myself where we used to walk together. I can't tell you now how many days did pass so. One day I start to feel so tired, I thought I woulda faint.

It happen close to the kutya, so I went inside and khukray in the corner facening the lingam and I start remembering how is right there in front a that lingam I did joray my hand inside a he one and pray that the circle a he protection would never break. How it happen is that one day the rain catch we near the kutya and we was running to it to get shelter. As we running, Stewart shoulder hit a laden branch a one a the frangipani tree and it break. Both a we stop same time because I think both a we probably feel sad in the same way when it happen, and then he break the branch off completely and tell me, "Run, run. We will make sure that it is a worthwhile accident."

When we get inside the gallery part of the kutya, he tell me, "Sit down. We have work to do." I laugh and siddown flat on the floor and start to loose out my hair so it will dry. He siddown next to me and ask, "Are you going to help me?" When I turn my head to see what he need me to do, I surprised to see that he splitting the base a each a the frangipani flower just a little bit, and not near either the petals or the end a the base, and then he thread another one into it and he keep on doing that until he get it long enough to bring the two ends together to make a mala. I help him when I understand what he doing and so we make two frangipani mala.

He get up and pull me up too, and then he put he hands on my shoulders just like he did do on the first first day he touch me. Then he ask me, "If I ask you to get married to me, would you say yes?" And I put my hands up and lock them around he neck and I say, "Yes, but Pandit Dan not here and I don't think he will do that for me a next time because he done do it once already." Then he ask me, "Do you remember when I told you that being here makes me think of Shakuntala and Dushyant?" I tell him I remember but I don't know them. He throw back he head and laugh and say, "I think you do, you know, but you just can't consciously remember that life. Their wedding was a Gandharva wedding. Do you know what a Gandharva marriage is?" I never hear about that, so he explain that it is the way the heavenly artists and many famous people like Shakuntala and Dushyant get marrid.

"All we need," he say, "is the presence of the Gods and two malas and we just made them. Today, we will be married in front of the immortal lovers, Shiv and Parvati." He take the malas from where he did hang them on the hooks on the gallery door frame and hand them to me. He open the door into the inside part of the kutya, raise he hand and ring the ghanta a few times, walk a few steps inside and ashtang karay in front a the lingam. Then he raise back up to he knees and siddown on he heels and say, "Mataji, Pitaji, I have found the one who complements me like both of you complete each other. Today we give thanks that you brought us together and come before you to exchange our garlands of flowers as a gesture of our acknowledgement that our love is eternal because it emanates from yours. Today we pledge our bonds to each other through all time and beg that you never stretch it so far again as to make life unbearable, as it has been until we met once again."

He stand up then, turn and put me to stand facing him so that both a we was standing sideways in front the lingam. He take one a the mala from me and say, "You have to put yours on me first." Then he put on the other one on for me. He move me to stand up in front a him with my back against he chest, which was my favourite position any time I with him, and he bring up the two a we hands with he own joray over mine and he tell me to talk to them in my mind for a little bit and then we will leave. That is how I always used to pray and how I does pray still, so it was easy for me to just fall in step with him. When he let me go, he move forward to light the deeya and make aarti and when I see what he doing, I put my right hand through the bend in he left elbow so we could offer it together like a real husband and wife.

The rain was still not over when we done, so he siddown with he back against the wall with one leg stretch out and the other one bend by the knee with he hand resting on he knee. I went and siddown with my back against the leg that he hand resting on and he start to tell me the story a Shakuntala and Dushyant while he hand was playing in my hair. That make me feel to drop asleep and I can't remember the story because that is exactly what happen, and when I wake up I did shift, or he did shift me, so that my head was under he chin and my face was resting against he chest. It didn't look like he sleep and as soon as I wake up, he tell me that we work still not done and the rain over so we could go do it now.

The work was to plant the frangipani branch that did break and while we doing that, we see a bargad just a few inches high trying to grow between some stones. I tell Stewart I want to take it out from there and plant it in a proper place and when he ask why, it was my turn to teach he. I explain that all the gods does live in that tree, and any troubles you have you could tell the tree and they will keep it a secret for you and help to take the troubles you tell them about away from you. He take the little plant out and we plant it in the middle between here and the shop. You could see the giant it is now if you look straight ahead through the window. The frangipani right next to the kutya is the one we did plant that day.

But I was telling you how I looking for Steward and how I started to feel like I going to faint. Was like them memories was more than my heart could bear and the blazing fire like it rip right through my belly, and the pain was so bad that I thought I woulda dead. Then I feel like if I peeing myself and I can't stop it. When I get up and pass my hand, I see that my clothes was soaking with blood, not water. I bawl and bawl and bawl and when I couldn't bawl no more I leave the kutya and walk down to the river and walk in to bathe with all my clothes on, even though I know you not supposed to go in the river or the sea when you in that condition. Now that I talking about it, I realise that that was also the one and only day that I didn't think about Baba warning about the river in rainy season.

While I was floating in the water, not caring where it carry me, even if is Guaracara River side or Oropouche River side or straight to the sea in the Gulf of Paria, which is where all a them will be heading anyhow you take it, I hear a voice saying, "Ma! Ma!" over and over again. I come up straight and when I watch on the bank where the sound was coming from, I see a little girl with curly hair watching me. Then she smile and wave at me. And she say, "Plans change for this lifetime, Maiya. But not for any others, and soon we will meet again." But after I throw myself in the water and start to swim to she, when I raise my head again, I couldn't see she nowhere.

But that is when I suddenly realise that it only had one thing for me to do. I had to go back to finish my life with Ganesh. Because Stewart decision and what that cause to happen to me did take away any other decision outta my hands. That is why my daughter make it she business to come and say what she say to me. So, even in the middle a my sadness, I realise that I was sure about one thing still. I went back home believing with all my heart that I carrying Stewart blessing with me, just as I sure he must be carry mine with he to Scotland, and I trust that the decision he make, he make only because he was thinking about what is best for me.

Afterwards, I had so much time to remind myself that that is how it is. Because really and truly, so many good things come outta that time with Stewart that I wish I could see him just once self to tell him thanks for all that he do for me. For one thing, I did start to blame Ganesh for the fact that I wasn't making baby. I try everything I could try and nothing wasn't happening. When I tell Miss Mildred about it, she tell me about Siparie Mai what some other people does call La Divina Pastora. Miss Mildred make all the arrangements for a taxi to carry me there one day, so that I could make a offering to the mother. She say the mother don't refuse you nothing you ask for. But like the mother refuse to help me with my problem. I did start to think about how the same thing did happen to Ganesh Dada. I suppose is just because I didn't want to take the blame on myself, I thinking how he side family really never had plenty children anyhow. I did start to think that them must have a serious family problem for that to happen. But my time with Stewart make me realise that the problem might be with me because I never could find a way, even when I try my best, to be with Ganesh like I used to be with Stewart. We time together and everything else that come and happen after make me realise that maybe nobody didn't really have no problem at all. Nobody wasn't without blame. And it didn't have no blame to lay on nobody. The world is just what it is, nothing more, nothing less. Once I understand that and I go back Fuente Grove with Ganesh, I start to treat the time me and Ganesh spend together different, just like how I does live my life up to today.

I couldn't teach Ganesh how to walk up behind me and surprise me by smelling like a ramgoat and make me feel excited one time, or how to make my heart beat so hard that I would get deaf and dizzy, but I did have enough confidence in my own self now to move Ganesh hands where I want them to be and to put something in he mouth when I want it to be and other little things like that. And if I find that he ain't coming in my room, but I feeling like I want to be with he, then I used to just go across to he room. While we did remain together, he never once say he don't want me to do that, so it work out well for we.

Sometimes I used to fall asleep and spend the night, and I used to like that because is such a natural thing to sleep with other people. You does feel somehow safer and you does fall asleep easier and dream better. But most times I used to prefer to come back in my bed to sleep when I ready. The new me make both me and Ganesh happier than we used to be before I leave, and I feel that if it wasn't for this, when Ganesh take up massaging he mighta be a far worse massager than he turn out to be, and we wouldn't a be able to make a way in life for we self at all, at all.

If the way things turn out telling me the truth about it, I think that maybe, up to now, if he does think about it at all, Ganesh must still chalk up the new ways we did start to come together to the fact that we was separate for such a long time, although not as long as this time that he leave me, instead of me leaving he. To tell you the truth, I did stop to wonder now and again, eh, about what he really know deep in he heart, and if he admit to heself what he know when he dedicate he autobiography many years later to Lord Stewart of Chichester as his friend and counsellor.

I also sure that if was Stewart I did go to Fuente Grove with, the fountain he used to cause to spring up in me, because we belong together naturally, and he know how to touch me, because he like touching me just as much as I did like it, and like doing it to he, my life woulda be a different story altogether. Fuente Grove mighta been a grove a fountains in a different way than Ganesh and me make it become after I went back there to live with him. But that story was never meant to be. The only one I have is the one in which I live for a while with Ganesh as the Mystic Masseur's Wife, as Mrs Leela Ramsumair, which is how Ganesh start to call me from time to time, although most of the times it was still just Leela or Leela girl.

But besides the money, which was very useful for living the life I had was to go back to, I also always carry the poem Stewart write for me and I does still draw strength from it whenever I feel myself getting tired. I did hand Pa the envelope with the money and never watch the envelope again after that, but I take the poem back to Fuente Grove with me and I know is that what make me the best mystic masseur wife I coulda ever be – the best Leela Ramsumair. I still have that poem. Look it here:

How do I Love Thee?

I love you because I love you.
Neruda knows about that
Even Shakespeare and all.
I understand their terms well.
But they haven't said what I know
When I knew that I love you
Have loved you forever
And always will …

Glorious Love

I love you
Because no gain
No profit is involved.
You are my gift from a caring universe.
I love you because your existence enchants me.
Because you can seduce me
With just a look.

I love you when you laugh
When you're thoughtful or worried
When you share your rage and ambitions and hopes
When you cry
When you are sweaty
From walking up high hills to find me
When I see you trying to make a place for yourself
In a world that is so hostile.

I love you
When you go bravely into spaces that make no room for you,
When you refuse no-entry signs
That threaten to drag you down when you try to fly.
I know I love you
Because when you enter a place
Even if I haven't seen you
I feel your presence.
I know you like I know no other.

I love you when I hear your voice
It envelops me inside and out
I love you because when I think of you, I smile.
When I know I am going to see you I bathe and dress,
And whatever the radio plays I sing loudly along.

I feel happy way, way, deep inside.
It shows on the outside.
Others see it too because I look different.

They feel it because I am good to be around
When I have been with you.

I know I love you
Because when I see you
I want to sit close to you
To touch you, to hold you
To wrap myself around you
With my breath, my thoughts, my eyes.

I love you because I don't contend with facts
That you eat, fart, shit, sleep,
And snore, slurp and slobber;
That you will dry up, age and die.
I love you because you're not perfect
You walk like a duck
And have strange growths on your body

Quotidian love

I love you
Like my cigarettes
Which fill my lungs
Sting my blood and kick me in the brain
And let me daily cope a while.
When I must go on just a little longer,
I love you like my cigarette.

I love you like dirt
That leaves a hint
Of bitter clay on the tip of my tongue,
And coats it
For many hours long.

I love you like chewing gum
With its burst of flavour
That can never last forever.

Green love

I love you
So I created one out of two.

When to keep dreams, fears, desires secret
You planted a pipaad,
And I had to plant one on top of yours
Because I thought your sapling would die,
Exposing your secrets to the world,
In secret I planted another
Right next to the dying.
You need never know, I think.

They both flourish
And now no one can tell
To which this branch or that belongs
For whom this leaf or that shines
No one can tell that once there were two.
I love you
Because you planted in me a pipaad tree

As you could probably see from that, Stewart was the real writer, the one I know best and could understand most clearly, the one with the most important things to say to me. He was a real Brahman, just like Baba, a man who could speak he own truth and nobody else one, in he own way always. Baba used to say, "Bayti you must know a real Brahman when you meet one because that one will only ever act when the time is right – never before and never after. The only thing that real Brahman people interested in is listening to what is inside a them and finding the best way to bring that outside. That is their job. Nothing more and nothing less. You have to be your own person. You have to trust the fact that you belong in your own skin. When people following fashion, when them doing thing just to look good in other people eye, when they making thing up against all parampar, it does make me shame when people does call them Brahman."

Anybody with one eye self coulda see that Stewart is the kinda person that Baba was talking about.

I wish with all my heart that one part a the blessing had been the pretty dogla baby that I did start to feel forming, but that was not to be.

I spend a whole fortnight by Pa, crying over what I did lose and could never have again and trying to catch myself. And I hold onto that poem for man and god. It give me a centre from which to be who I did become after. Once or twice during the fortnight, I did think that I would just stay with Pa and never go back. I had the money to do that and more if I did need to live so. But then I realise that that would just turn everybody life upside down for no good reason, and that self is what Stewart did realise for he own self before he leave that money to make sure I alright and went away. I did know that Ganesh happy with Beharry and he new book and that he think that I only gone for a little bit and go come back soon. So I give myself that little time to catch myself before I get up and go back to become the mystic masseur's wife.

CHAPTER 5: THE LIFE OF
THE MYSTIC MASSEUR'S WIFE

Is only when I reach back Fuente Grove after I stop looking for Stewart that I realise how much trouble and how little gain that one book Ganesh write would really mean for we. One thousand a them Ganesh print, and except for the one or two we give away, we had to find something to do with all the rest. Until Ganesh get famous, that was a next task to add to my list. First first, Beharry put them in he shop to sell! You ever hear more schupidness? Fellas who could hardly read going to Beharry rum shop just to get drunk on a Saturday, and their wife going to buy alu, dal, saltfish, flour and rice on the next side, and these two fools think a book with philosophical question and answer go sell in that place!

When that eh work and Ganesh carry the book to the book-shops and even some ordinary shops, plenty a them turn it down point blank, and the one or two who willing to consider it want a fifteen-cent commission on every copy. In fact, over the next few years it was only my common sense that save we from the book madness that did threaten to ruin we life. Sometimes I used to think that I had was to pick up from where other people did reach in helping Ganesh out with he life, from he mother who dead, to give him life onwards. But not me alone.

I saying this because it was with the big book failure that Fyzabad Phua, who Ganesh did secretly start to call The Great Belcher, because she did develop a bad wind problem, come in once again to put a hand on he to move him in the right direction. This was after about six months of we catching we tail by we self, with Ganesh going from place to place trying to sell the book. I did get to like Fyzabad Phua so much, you hear, which was the name all a we used to call she to she face, since I first first meet she until

91

the day she dead. But that particular day she visit, me and she did nearly fall out, and it had other times, too, when this same kinda thing did happen, all because a Ganesh. But that day it happen because I think that she was taking Ganesh side and I worrying about how much longer we could go on so with Ganesh feeling like he not accomplishing nothing useful with what he putting so much work in.

Baba used to say that a man don't feel like a man unless he know how to make the right moves to stay on top a he world. Baba, just like he sister, didn't mind lending a hand to help a man to do that. So I was glad Phua did come because it didn't have no move that Ganesh was making in them days that was looking right to me. On top a not making no money, it had the law firm taking what little bit we getting. Ganesh used to have to go to the bank in San Fernando all the time to take out from the oil royalty money to pay them. Every time he come back, he used to tell me that the lawyers must be working because up to now the money still coming in the account every month.

He used to put a few dollars in the tin what we did bring from Four Ways with the kitcheree money and what Pa give me. I really never count what Stewart leave for me, and when Pa start handing me back that money quiet quiet after he change it, I start to put that and all in the pan. I keep on using it for all we expenses, without Ganesh suspecting nothing, but still, I didn't know how long it woulda last and I know Ganesh feeling the pressure. Sometimes I used to get vex when it seem that Ganesh think people could live on air. Like he think I don't spend no money to buy and cook food for we, to mind the cows and the chickens, to make the little garden and make sure we have clothes, curtains, bedsheet and pillowcase and thing to keep we and the place presentable and clean.

I think the first thing what get me vex that day when Fyzabad Phua visit was when she did try to convince we that a man name Bissoon, who all a we except Ganesh know in different, and for me not so good ways, shoulda try to sell that first book. And when Bissoon come to we house, and pick up the book from the floor where he did sitting down, he leave it there after he look at it. Then he look around at all a we and declare that he handle plenty poetry already, and it go surprise all a we to know how much people in Trinidad does write poetry, and he handle essays and thing, but he never handle a cyatechism before and he eh think he really want to try. Phua didn't like that at all and she work on him to bring him around and I watching she and admiring what she doing. But then Bissoon ask for nine cents commission, and bold bold he telling Phua that he reminding she that if any sort a printed matter could sell in Trinidad, she know he is the man to sell it.

But is when Bissoon tell she he go take thirty books to start off, that I get vex. I didn't agree with that nine cents if was for only thirty a them, and I open my mouth to say so and remind them that the book shops did offer we fifteen for all. But before I could finish two-three sentence good, Phua cut me off and say to Bissoon, "Yes man, we know you have a hand. You is the man who go sell the books for my boy Ganeshwa here." When Bissoon gone, I reminding them that is this Bissoon self what Pa keeping in he mind because Bissoon sell him all a them books he didn't really want to buy. Bissoon did say, "They is American books. Pretty books. Nice books. Is the fastest-selling books I ever handle and this is the last set. If you get it, you is a lucky man, Ramlogan."

But Phua cut she eye at me and tell me that she don't know how I could be a shopkeeper daughter because, like, I can't count too good. She say, "Leela, you can't see that Bissoon offer we a better deal than the bookshop and it eh have no bookshop what woulda take all. Like you really don't know nothing about business." And she end off with, "Leela, Bissoon come here to sell Ganesh book, not yours." As if I didn't know that. And what was worse, she ask me if is so I does support my husband, as if I ever do anything else besides support my husband. When I start to tell she so, Ganesh cut in. He laugh and say, "Chutanwalay choot lay jaye. Sas patohiya ekay hoye." That really shut me up. But me and Phua was really always one in all those years because, if only for Baba sake, we did only always want whatever is the best for Ganesh.

Ganesh stop quiet for a little bit, and then he say, "Is a sign. Anybody who could sell a book to your father could sell milk to a cow. And Bissoon going to get that book sell for me." I watch him looking so hopeful, and I just had was to stop quarrelling one time. I say, "You right, you know. Bissoon sell them books to Pa. Is them books that you see in the shop that make you interested in we. They put the idea a authoring in your head because you holding one when Pa ask you what you going to do with your life, and you answer him that you going to write plenty book like the one you have in your hand. You do what you say and now is the same Bissoon who selling them for you. Is a sign for true."

As it happen, Bissoon couldn't sell the books, even though Ganesh did start to think that he woulda achieve big important things after he write that cyatechism, as Bissoon call it. Bissoon tell we afterwards that the trouble with the book was that it was really a little too early for the state a things in this place. He say, "Is the sort of book you go have hell even giving away because people go think you want to work some sign a magic on them." And that is a big problem for we, eh. That people don't really understand who is we, and plenty a them fraid we, and plenty more hate we because they don't know nothing about we at all. Ganesh did include one or two everyday mantras in the book and give each one a nice name like *Prayer to Wake up* and *Prayer to Go to Sleep* but then underneath that he did write the mantras in Sanskrit and that mighta frighten some people. They coulda mistake it for mystical magic in truth, and if they superstitious they wouldn't a want to have a book like that in their house at all, at all.

But since the book wasn't selling, it couldn't make no money for we and I had to insist that Ganesh take up the massaging so that he could sense the value a he own life. I do that because Pa always used to say that Baba used to do massage so good, although I could never remember Baba doing any massaging in the ten years I did know him. But you know how much trouble Ganesh give we before he say yes? He say, "What this place need with a next massager? You know how much a them it have around this place?" And that was another reason I didn't like that Beharry fella. Because I did know that that wasn't really Ganesh talking. It was Beharry.

I hear that with my own ears when Ganesh tell him he going to take up massaging and Beharry start discouraging him one time. "Man, you choose a hard hard thing. These days nearly everybody you bouncing up is either massager or dentist. One of my own cousin – really Suruj Mooma cousin, but Suruj Mooma family is like my own family – a really nice boy he is, he too starting in this thing." After that, we really had to try hard to reason with Ganesh. Phua say, "Yes, but it need plenty massagers in this place because so much people does be sick all the time and it ain't have nobody to care for them, Ganeshwa. Them doctor and them don't know nothing about how to cure Trinidad people problem you know, far less Fuente Grove people, and they does charge a set a money if you even walk inside their office by mistake; these people does do robbery with V – without blinking their eye."

When we still couldn't convince him, we remind him about how good Baba was at it, but when we say that, well...! He say, "Allyuh feel I is my father? Well, never forget that I is not he and never forget about that girl who did dead after he rub she." But I did never hear about that, and Phua say not to take him on because the gift had to be running in his blood. But it didn't work out to be so at all. Anybody come with any trouble, Ganesh like he ain't really want to touch them. When he do touch them he treating them so rough that they complaining. And then he end up just telling all a them the very same thing, no matter what the problem is that they come with: "You just have a little bad blood. Nothing wrong with you. Nothing at all."

So you asking me what my husband was like as a massager. Well, in my opinion, Ganesh mighta be a much better one if he did know how to respect the human body in the proper way. But from the things Ganesh say from time to time, I feel that maybe because he mother dead when he did so young, or maybe Baba didn't hug him up and thing too much, seeing as how he is a boy, or maybe is all a them book he reading; I don't know what it is but I used to think that Ganesh never really understand what it is to have a body. And when I say that, as you know, I saying plenty. But he had much better luck as a mystic and we shoulda realise the potential he had for that all the time, insteada trying to make him take up massaging. But is so life is sometimes, right? Sometimes it does be hard to remember that a person is their own person and you have to respect all that person various parts. And then again, if it wasn't for the failure a the massaging, we couldn't a get to that point.

But it was plenty plenty thing I had to put up with before we get to the point when he did get fame as a mystic. I remember how much rude children we had to deal with. One time a boy mother bring him with a mash-up shin bone. While we examining the boy self, the child say as boldface as you please, "But what happen that all you people looking at me so for? I kill priest?" The mother self ain't even buff him for being so rude to big people. Instead she say, "Look at this boy! You think he make for any rough game?" I was about to tell she that he look like he does be very rough on everybody and she should try not to spoil him too much, when the mother start explaining. She say, "Look at my crosses. One day I see the boy coming home limping. I say, what happen that you limping, boy? He answer me back brave brave like a man, 'I was playing football.' I say, 'Playing the fool, you mean.'" Well I understand right away where he get he rudeness from and didn't have to ask no more questions.

It had one good thing Ganesh used to do when he was seeing people in pain, and I think that was the beginning a the mystic shining through, although I still don't know what make he think to do it. It was when I make the fresh coconut oil, he used to make me boil piece piece a all the grass and leaf that growing around Fuente Grove in the oil and he use it to rub on wherever people say they having a pain and then he give a little bit to the people to carry home so that they could do it for their self. In no time, people start to talk about the miracles that this oil perform for them. I suppose it help that while Ganesh rubbing it he used to chant:

Zindagi ki rooh tha
Roohaniyat ki sham tha
Woh mujassam roop mein
Insan kay irfan tha

I think some people find that very impressive, even if some a them get frighten.

But Ganesh was really like a blind earthworm, if you ask me, burrowing through life, and when that rude boy and he mother come, I think Ganesh get so flabbergasted by the lady bullying ways that he say, "Drink it" instead a "Rub it." It didn't do he reputation or we one for that matter much good, I could tell you that. Although if the child did have constipation they mighta thank we for it. But you know, is probably the blindness that cause Ganesh to finally find a place for heself in this world.

Just so just so, one day, after the incident with the lady and she son, he was in Beharry shop as usual and Beharry hand him something he get from Everyman Library. He and Beharry nearly fall out bad that day over that Everyman, because Beharry start to do for heself what Ganesh feel like he teach him to do, which is to send away for thing they see in advertisement. But Ganesh tell me afterwards that he forget he rage right away because he get so interested in what the catalogue offering. And you done know how he woulda have to make that into a big thing. "The interest in good things in a man's heart is what does keep him from involving heself in bad things," he say in the mystic voice he did start to work on, although I sure it was without really realising what he doing.

Then, one evening, when he come home and start measuring the drawing room walls, I feel so happy. I thinking, "Prabhu, you work in mysterious ways in true. Just so just so, this man looking to make some improvements to this house." But then Ganesh say he looking to see how much shelf he go have to build because he send for all the books in the catalogue. I start to cry so, eh, that I couldn't stop. For days I cry. I cry when the big van come from the post office and we had to spend nearly the whole day emptying all a them books and carrying them to put on the bookshelf Ganesh build. I crying all the time while we going from the van to the shelf, from the shelf to the van.

But you know, I think is because people in the village see how this man dedicated to the reading thing that they finally start to respect we. Up to that point, we was just strange new people what move in their village who they can't understand at all, even though I used to say good morning or Walekum Salam or Sitaram to them when I bringing and carrying out DeviDoy and going and coming back from my sewing class. After that day, people start to come to ask for Ganesh help with all kinda reading and writing business and that is how we become part a the village. It help, too, when they come and see how we living, that even though they never see no pandit coming in we house, we living the kinda life a pandit woulda bless we for.

And then it so happen that Ganesh and Beharry start to read *Gita* together, and when people come for help with their reading and writing business, Ganesh start giving them a little bit a philosophy for living their life too, and that is how Ganesh start up with being the mystic. It make for another set a book buying, but at least this time he start to use what he did learning from the book to help people to understand their self and their situation. The *Gita* reading make him learn how to read deeper, which was one good thing Beharry did encourage him to do. But this is another time me and Fyzabad Phua did nearly fall out, because she always want me to be more quiet than I coulda ever be, although she was right to tell him that he just scratching, and that scratching, when all is said and done, is not hoeing and it wouldn't make nothing grow.

But I was getting older and wiser, so rather than quarrelling with Phua I put on a crying instead – and I admit all my crying after the real crying Stewart cause was pretend crying, oui. I do it just to make people see I not too pleased with what was going on. This time was because I did have a idea, when I see how Ganesh helping the people them when they come to see him, but I didn't know how to say it to him. So, after Phua tell him about just scratching, I say, "That self I telling him, Phua, and I telling him he should do panditaye. He know so much more than any a them pandit it have around here, anyhow. Is high time he become a pandit, Phua."

Well, like that light a fire in she. She start to tell Ganesh about the kinda powers he father and he father father and he father father father and so on down the line did have to cure people soul. By the time she done with he, he was a humble man for once, and for the first time since I come back to Fuente Grove, I feel a little happy.

Afterwards, I think how it was the falling out Phua did have with she righthand woman – who she did nickname King George

— that put so much force in the way she talk to Ganesh. I didn't ask she nothing, but I know Phua did meet this lady at a wedding and she was so impressed by how this woman take charge a everything in the place, that when she find out that she didn't have no place to go back to, she give she the name King George and take she under she wing. After that, everything Phua doing and everywhere she going, King George going with she. And then King George fall hard for a married man in Arouca and stop being with Phua. That is all I know and I didn't feel it was my place to ask more question. Was a thing into which nobody didn't have the right to enquire.

Much later, Ganesh write about how Phua make him who he is in one a he book and I really did like how he describe the gift a Poopha books what Phua give him the next fortnight after she convince him that he have the Powers. Watch here:

> A fortnight later my aunt from Fyzabad brought a parcel wrapped in red cotton spattered with sandalwood paste and handed it over to me with all the appropriate ceremony. When I untied the parcel I saw books of many sizes and many types. All were in manuscript, some in Sanskrit, some in Hindi; some were of paper, some of palm strips. The palm strips bound together looked like folded fans.

I think it was the advice she give him though, more than Poopha books, that make Ganesh truly and finally turn mystical. That was the biggest turning point in Ganesh life and since I was supposed to be he wife after all, it was a kinda big thing for me too. Phua tell him that he have to believe in the people who come to see him. He cannot doubt what they trying to tell him about what they experience. She say, "Is them life, and is them who know it best. Never doubt that. If you don't understand what them trying to say, you have to question them quiet quiet until they and you understand what the problem coulda be. But you can't never think that they don't know what they talking about. When they finish talk, and you understand what they telling you about they troubles and pains, you have to meditate on what they say to find out what is the right answers that they must receive. In this way, they will know that you believe in them and they will believe in you always."

For the rest of we days in Fuente Grove, I watch Ganesh put this piece a magic into practice and I did pleased to watch how he become a man Baba woulda be proud to call he son, because now he was a humble man, a man willing and able to listen to what other people have to say. I hope that I, too, did become a little like that alongside him.

Fyzabad Phua recommend a little advertising to let people know about the new mystical business. But you wouldn't believe, or maybe you would, because it have so much people like that all about these days, that when he went by Basdeo, the man with the printery who doing printing for Ganesh since we wedding, instead a accepting what Ganesh heself write about in the pamphlet that he design heself too, Basdeo start to yap about he own ideas. Ganesh say that after that, Basdeo start shaking he head over the pamphlet, saying, "Tell me nah man, just tell me, how people does get so crazy in a small small place like Trinidad?"

That is the problem we have in this country, where people don't have no respect for other people capability and what they trying to do. The only person they interested in is their own self, unless they sick and fall down and in need, in which case they does start to run after any and everything to cure the worries and pain. They like douen, nah, and when Phua turn Ganesh away from how he was, she prevent him from being like them other people who foot going in one direction and they head facing the next.

And if you think I lie, when I tell you that with Bissoon it was the same thing, you must believe me. Phua did willing to forgive Bissoon after that, but not me. I wouldn't a forgive him up to today if he didn't come to such a bad end and had to go to one a the same kinda old people home what we hear Kaka did have to beg them to take him in. Phua forgive Bissoon long before that. I suppose is because she wasn't like me and she didn't see Basdeo or Bissoon refusal as a reflection on the value a what Ganesh was going to be doing. She say, "Oh don't worry nah, man. Bissoon ain't what he used to be. He losing he hand, ever since he wife run away with Jhagru, the Siparia barber, four, five, six months now. And mind you this Jhagru was a married man, you hear, with six children! Just like King George man. Bissoon telling every Tom, Dick and Harrylal that he go kill Jhagru, but he ain't doing nothing. He just start drinking, like all them other man in he position."

Phua was right. You can't concern yourself with what a man like that thinking. In fact, they shoulda make a song about he. I could hear it right now in the tune them young boy does sing in these days:

Rum is my lover, boy.
Rum is my lover.
You only have to say rum
And I will come over

I take on this fair lover
When everybody gone
She is a faithful
And very honest friend

Rum is my lover, boy
Rum is my lover
You only have to say rum
And I will come over

What the other man do
That I couldn't do
What make she leave me
And go with he for true

I thought she woulda come back
Come back for good
But like she like he six chirren
What nobody should

Rum is my lover, boy
Rum is my lover
You only have to say rum
And I will come over

That is a good one, eh? Hahaha! Sometimes I does feel like I could give them young people like Sundar Popo a run for their money in the composition business, oui.

But you didn't come to hear me sing. I was telling you about Phua and how she did finish up she story in she usual way. She say, "Too besides, Ganeshwa, you is a modern educated man and I think you should do things in a modern way. Put a advertisement in the papers, man, and call that George." I was glad to see Phua was strong enough to *say* George so much time without getting chest pain, because I still couldn't do it if anybody did say Stewart – and I never say that word myself in them days, not once – I would a start to feel sick one time. I feel like maybe he gone now to where we carry we true true name and that is why I does be able to say it a little bit easier now. And I feel that as soon as I get ready to go, he will come back and be waiting for me when is time for me to cross over.

But to come back to the explanation about what was going on on this side, I have to say nothing don't come easy for some people in this life, eh. And Ganesh didn't have no success for the first few months after the advertisement, and I telling you, it was in them few months that I start admiring Ganesh as much as I does still do. Nobody didn't come to see him for he spiritual services, even after he follow Phua advice and write in the papers that people could come for help. As for me, I get more work to do because, even though nobody ain't coming, he decide to build a shed in front the house to treat the people when they do start to come.

I did think he mad to do that when he ain't seeing nobody coming, although I never tell him so and I was glad that I keep quiet when it turn out that he did doing the right thing. The shed building was a month-long project and then, afterwards, working to help he out start up for me, for true. And I had to admire how hard he was trying when he feel like he on he true path. Some a the books used to have to go in the shed in the day and come back in the house in the night, and that did bound to include all the copies a *Questions and Answers*. Sometimes I used to just leave them outside because it didn't have nobody to take up any a them, and I did sure that nobody wouldn't a want them. Me and Ganesh fall out over that, but I didn't take he on. I continue to leave them outside when I feeling too tired to bring them in when night come. It wasn't as though he ever help me to bring and carry. I thinking, who in Fuente Grove go want to thief book?

Plenty people in Trinidad was making good money in them days, and not all a them was doing it in the terrible way that Kaka try to do it, because the Americans was here that time and even in Fuente Grove you coulda see one or two a the kinda dollars with the picture a the man who look like a lady. One or two time when I get tired bringing and carrying, I ask Ganesh why he can't get a real job with the Americans so he could make some real dollars, but I did feel sorry I say that after we hear about Kaki story. So is a good thing he didn't used to take me on neither.

One time, though, he take a turn in Beharry arse on the very day me and Beharry did see eye to eye on something. But I did realise by that time that sometimes you does really have to push a little bit when you dealing with Ganesh. And like is that self what Beharry and Phua did know from the start. So Beharry still tell him what he had to tell him, what he doing wrong and what he doing right, and after that incident everything finally start to straighten out good for we in the mystic business.

What happen is this. One day, Ganesh tell Beharry – and report back to me that he tell him, "It have a damn long time now you judging me like some blasted magistrate, and telling me where I going wrong. I read a lot a psychology book about people like you, you know. And what them book have to say about you ain't nice, I could tell you that." That put Beharry in he place, but not once and for all, because Beharry was never a easy one to keep there, no matter who telling him where that place is. So he still tell Ganesh what we did agree he have to tell him and that was about the way Ganesh used to dress.

"If you want to be a certain somebody," Beharry say, "then you have to learn to look like the certain somebody. When people understand that, it does take them a long way to being what they want to be, you hear." By some miracle, Ganesh listen and I self tie the first paghri on for he the very next morning. And is a interesting thing, because the day I put on paghri for Ganesh, the fact that I woulda have to lose my ganghri was clear, even though I didn't know that yet and woulda doubt anybody who did try to tell me so. Trinidad and Tobago never see nothing like this Ganesh before that day in 1941, and soon it didn't have nobody who coulda hold a candle to the Rishi and he wife, which is how people did start to talk about we afterwards.

On that very day when Ganesh put on that paghri, we had a client who come with a very serious mystical case about a big black cloud chasing she son. If it wasn't for Phua teaching, I don't know if Ganesh woulda be able to handle it at all but as it is, Ganesh do a very very good job. I will never forget how Ganesh deal with that case. In fact, I did get frighten when he walking up and down, up and down after the lady gone and whole night he praying over the case. It make me bawl at him, "I don't know why you wasting all this time on one little black boy for nah." I feel shame after I done say that; I know I behaving dotish just because I was so worried. Even Beharry look like he get a little frighten and vex too, because Ganesh not telling none a we what he thinking. He treat the case very private and very serious. But is so I come to see for myself how a man could let he own pain show him how to deal with other people one.

The lady did tell Ganesh the situation with the cloud and that is how come he did prepare for the boy fear, but she didn't tell him the part about shame, and like she didn't understand what the fear was really for and how it connect up with shame. She come by we because a she own fear and shame that the boy might end up in the mad house, because she well know that if you going mad house or gaol and you think you going in normal and will come back out normal, you damned wrong. Ganesh see that the biggest problem that child had was how much he did fraid that people was laughing at him. And as I realise many years afterwards, who better than Ganesh to understand how people laughing could hurt? Right away he recognise what going on and he put the boy at ease by making sure the boy understand that nobody by we laughing at him or will ever laugh at him.

What did happen to the boy is this. The mother send the boy, almost about a year before when they come by we, to buy some ice. He send he brother Adolphus instead and Adolphus get crushed against a wall by a army truck that couldn't negotiate the roads in Belmont where them living, because the driver lost control coming around a sharp corner on the narrow road. Adolphus was coming back with the ice when it happen and the boy see the whole thing happening to he brother and like he can't get what he see outta he mind. Like he brain freeze in terror at that moment nah, and he can't forget how the blood running from the body and the water running from the ice and they joining and mixing together and flowing away from the scene a this horror.

But the bigger problem was this. Many religion in this country don't do nothing to give support to the spirit before it come into and after it come outta the body. I feel like these people did belong to one a them group because the mother and father did well dress up and they had the boy nice and clean and looking good. But outside niceness is no protection against most thing eh, especially not bad timing death. And like the confused spirit a the dead child start clinging onto he brother and because the boy don't have no spiritual ability he can't see that it is he brother. He just seeing a changing black shape what he calling a cloud and he sensing that the cloud trying to pull him along into the other world. To kill him in other words – which is what he telling he mother and Ganesh.

Ganesh realise one time that what might also be wrong with this child was the guilt he feeling about the fact that is he brother and not he who come and dead. To cure that, Ganesh become a child heself to turn that child back into one, to make him feel that everything going to be alright and that he could chase away the dangerous killing form a this black cloud. He think is the guilt that did cause the brother spirit to take that shape in the boy mind. And then he used Poopha *Antyeshti Samskar* book to do a pitr puja to make sure that the dead boy will find he way on the other side and let go he brother on this side. That was one thing, eh, that you couldn't a ever fault Ganesh for, until we went to live in town, and he skip it for a few years until Pa come and dead, and he realise you could do puja wherever you is, no matter what. But before and after that, just like Baba, he used to perform pitr puja every year to make sure the debts to the ancestors and to the past and future getting paid every year, and this time he do it for this boy and he family.

People don't know all the details a the case. I think is the first time anybody ever siddown and describe it like how I doing it for you today, because I sure Ganesh never talk about it to nobody.

I telling you what I understand, because I was right there and he ask me to do one or two thing to help him and I figure out for myself what he doing and thinking. He never ever talk about any a he case to nobody, and even Beharry, who did get vex just like me when he wasn't telling we nothing about the first one, afterwards, did get accustom to that fact.

But in truth, even if he did tell people, plenty a them wouldn't a know how to make sense a what he saying. But that first case take Trinidad by storm. A lady tell me one time that she read a book what try to describe what Ganesh do (somebody riding on we success from the very beginning), and it sound to me that what the person hear is that we do something like in a gypsy circus. Well, I was there, and no circus didn't come to town that day or any other day after that too besides.

Plenty plenty people come after that with their troubles and most a them had that same kinda problem with the restless spirits a dead people holding onto them, family members who did gone to the other side but couldn't find their way, and that was always a simple matter for Ganesh to deal with. Now any pandit at all coulda help out these people same way eh, but Ganesh did get a reputation as a specialist in that area among people who woulda never think about consulting a pandit, because only one or two a the people he do thing for used to call him pandit. I lost count a the thousands and can't remember most a the case Ganesh did work on after that first boy, far less remember details about them. Ganesh cut out what one a the newspapers did say about him in them days and I still have it. Hear what they write:

Other thaumaturges who swarm all over Trinidad know an ineffectual charm or two but have neither the intelligence nor sympathy for anything else. Ganesh has elevated the profession by putting the charlatans out of business. But more than his powers, learning, or tolerance, people like Ganesh's charity. He has no fixed fee and accepts whatever is given him. When someone complains that he is poor and at the same time is persecuted by an evil spirit, Ganesh takes care of the bad spirit and waives the fee.

When the newspapers start saying thing so, we know Ganesh reach.

It only have four other thing I remember from that time that I think is important to tell you. One is when the fella name Basdeo, who print the first set a copies a *Questions and Answers* come and offer to reprint the book and to show Ganesh how to sell off what he did have. When he do it over and bring it come eh, that was a big shock and revelation to me. The new book did look pretty for true and thick and tall like a real book, nothing at all like how it did look like a copy book the first time. And I still can't believe how the same book that wasn't selling when it did first write, start selling like hot bread because the writer was a famous man now. Even Bissoon come to ask if he could get some to sell, but Basdeo did take over the marketing by that time and we didn't need Bissoon, who did end up break up and feeble, kinda sankaha really, because he wife did never come back.

But if Ganesh eh make mistake, he name wouldn't a be Ganesh. That is the second thing I does remember still. When it happen, to tell you the truth, I did actually think that it was the biggest mistake he coulda ever make. Let me tell you what that man do. The man take all the money what we did start making good good now, and he buy over Basdeo Printery not because he want to take away Basdeo job. No, no, not at all. Basdeo continue to run the place and he must be running it still for all I know; Ganesh buy it just so he could change the name on the outside to Ganesh Publishing Co. Ltd, Port of Spain – although the building in San Fernando. He say how he want any future book he write to have he own publishing company name on it.

Hot and sweaty as usual when he just done buy the printery, he print one book in it – he autobiography and he put a price on it – two dollars and forty cents, which was plenty money in them days, and then he telling me we could siddown and wait for the dollars – with the man who look like a lady – to start rolling in. When me eh seeing none a them dollars, he say, "Oh it selling well in Central America and all across the Caribbean because is a spiritual thriller and a metaphysical whodunit."

My arse! They reading a book in English in place where they does talk Spanish? He really think I schupid for true. And what the hell is meta whatever done it? I so vex that he spend so mucha we money that I thinking that *my* autobiography woulda be a more interesting book, because Ganesh never do nothing in them days besides what I encourage him to do. I was sure that a lot a people in this country just like me and wouldn't ever read anything like that, so it wasn't worth the money Ganesh had to spend to make it happen. That was how I was thinking about what he do. And I feel I had a right, because to publish that one big book nearly cause all we money what he coulda lay he hands on to go down the drain. That was in 1942. But that is what I mean by telling you that Ganesh is a earthworm. Because that same publishing company turn around and become the tool that we use to fight the evil that start to surround we. What a battle that follow for the next seven and a half years, eh! Them was years that I still don't know how to describe, because it take we clean outta the world I did know. But let me tell you about the other two thing I remember, before I give you the details a the bacchanal about that one.

The third thing was what really start to bring in some steady money for we. It was when we make a investment in a taxi service because Ganesh did get vex that Pa make the first investment in taxi and was charging people what Ganesh feel was too much to go to and from Fuente Grove. I sure the fellas Pa hire to drive the taxis he buy must be glad when he had the business sense to do that, but I didn't argue with Ganesh when he get on about it. It just make me frighten that he was starting to feel that he better than other people and know better than them what to do, how to do it and when to do it.

But as it turn out, I didn't have too much reason to worry, because when Ganesh buy over the taxis from Pa, he give him a fair price and then he fix the fees per mile that passengers going to pay. Truth was, I was kinda suspecting that Pa mighta use my own money from Stewart to buy the taxis and I was very sorry when he get on with Ganesh as though Ganesh was taking out some kinda personal revenge on him. But in the end I was glad that Ganesh do what he do because that money did become the steadiest flow a all that we make, and like the rest a the money Ganesh make throughout he life, we did earn it fair and square.

And I come to think that with Pa way, it was really digging out needy people eye because, baychara, they was willing to pay anything you ask them, if they think they must come to see Ganesh to get he help for whatever troubling them. It was good because you could never tell how much people woulda give after they receive their counselling, but how this money was fix you was a little more sure about it.

The last thing was the most serious, and is how we come to get involved in the newspapers publishing business that did start to boom in Trinidad in them days, and how we start to cut track for we final end, even though we didn't have no idea at the time about what kinda end was waiting around that corner. The four news-papers what we used to buy when Ganesh start having a little throw-away money, and what we used to read because Ganesh used to bring them home from Beharry shop the day after Beharry done with them, was *The Trinidad Chronicle*, *The Trinidad Guardian*, *The Trinidad Palladium*, and *The Trinidad Sentinel*.

But then all of a sudden it had so much different, different kind he start bringing home – evening one, weekly one, monthly one, bimonthly one, annual one, you name it. It had one did name *The Indian: A Monthly Magazine* and another one did name *The Observer: An Organ of Indian Opinion*. And you did bound to know the Presbyterian one. Most a them use East Indian in their name. I remember *The East Indian Herald* and *The East Indian Weekly*. Ganesh say is all the fuss they making about the 1945 Centenary Celebration of Indian Arrival in Trinidad and Tobago that caus-ing everybody to want to jump in the party and say something about what it mean to be Indian that make him interested to read them, to make some kinda sense about what really going on.

Some a them was also reporting on all kinda thing what going on in the rest a the country and I remember that one a them did have a column call "Top a the charts", and it used to have the words for the one at the top. I used to cut them out and keep to sing along when they playing on the radio. I still have it in my song folder here. When Mildred come to stay with me, sometimes we does take it out, play the records with the songs and sing and dance and get drunk. It does always be real fun. If I remember correct, I think the same year it had all the centenary celebrations, that column did carry the words a one a the most popular songs that time. It was by Lord Invader and I remember it went:

Run your run Kaiser Wilhelm
Run you run
You hear what Churchill say
With a rope and a mango wood
We go fuck up Germany

And then there was this monthly one that bring a lot a trouble into we life. They did call that one *The Hindu*, and I feel that that is the one that do the most to help some Indian people to know that they name Hindu. Same time it also do the most to make people shame that they name Hindu because a how it used to carry a set a scandal, gossip and lies. Ganesh say it set a new low standard in Trinidad for newspaper publishing. Is Beharry what bring it for Ganesh to see because it had a scandalous column, named *A Little Bird Tells Us*. What Beharry wanted Ganesh to see was that somebody saying how Ganesh running taxi service now. "Is a new kind of mysticism, they sarcastically write in the papers," Beharry say, looking at Ganesh like if he want to cry.

But is only when Fyzabad Phua see it and come down Fuente Grove to tell Ganesh that Pa start to call him the Business Man of God – because a the taxi business what Pa did still vex about – that Ganesh wake up to the fact that he had to do something. Phua come to make sure Ganesh take action. When she put she two hand on she waist and ask him what he going to do about it, he didn't have no choice but to think hard about what to do before things could go from bad to worse. The trouble is that we did really end up being a very widespread business monopoly in true, even though that is not what we start out to do at all.

Is just that I start to cook so that people could get something to eat, because sometimes they coming from very early and they leaving late. So we end up in the restaurant business. Then again, Fuente Grove is a outta the way place so Beharry start to stock up on the things that people does need. They need things to do their puja and he add them to the rest a the new things that he did have to buy – the usual oil, flour, dal, rice, salt, sugar, alu and saltfish that he always have in the old shop. That old shop is what he turn into he and Suruj Mooma new grocery. They name it Surujdeo Grocers and put up a big sign with that name on the roof.

Then it had people who was coming from all over, even if they not doing puja their self. They was just bringing other people or just coming to watch the house a miracles, as some people start calling we house. And they did want more than a quick nip a the bad rum the poor canefield workers used to want on weekends. The rum the labourers used to drink was mainly puncheon rum like Life Preserver, Victory, and others that they used to call Lock-up-de-bitch and Beat-de-police, what the regular rumsuckers did like.

I remember them rum good from when I was a little girl, because men in front a Pa shop used to compare rum and rum price between Pa shop and Mr Chen and he wife Gumlin shop. I used to also use the rum bottles, especially the nip, to full gheew and sometimes the bigger bottles to full dahee and milk too. I have nothing against rum, as I tell you, and as a matter of fact, when we went Port of Spain to live, I did like the different different kinda drinks they used to make with rum in it, and me and Mildred develop a good hand to mix them. So back in the day, I used to just rinse out the bottles clean clean, and they was very good bottles, and free too, for me to put my products in. Now, because a different kinda people coming in the place, Beharry did have to do a little expansion to make a whole new rum shop.

Was the first one in the village like what they did have in San Fernando, with radio and plenty more space, so more people could come in and siddown by a table and drink plenty other thing besides rum at their leisure. Beharry make the new rum shop with four pairs a swinging saloon doors, with a big sign across the top a all the doors saying WELCOME FRIENDS in big big capital letters. He used to keep the rumshop dark like the ones in San Fernando, and he make a private inside room with table and chairs where more important people could siddown and eat and drink and talk, and he make a next room with radio and some billiard tables. Both a them rooms did have jalousie windows which was the style I used to see in San Fernando. Bhowji did have to get somebody to help she make the cutters for the rum shop, fuss the work did get to be too much for she. She used to make all kind a thing:

pholourie and chutney, pachaunie and sandwich and thing. When I see my first Western film, I realise that that is where the original rumshop pattern come from. Even the ones in San Fernando woulda also be design after the ones in the movies.

But Beharry was never one who did know where to draw a line, and like if that wasn't enough, he come and start having wrestling match and stick-fight competition in front a the rum shop every Saturday night saying how Gandhiji set the example of a good diet, good discipline and a good body. The first time he say that in my hearing, I nearly cuss. I thinking, "Is dotish he dotish to put Gandhiji and good body in the same sentence?" But whatever nonsense he saying, it was making very good money for he, and in them days people used to associate anything Beharry doing with we. Big big match, I telling you, with big big men coming from all over the country betting big big money. And, of course, we did have the fleet a taxi what I tell you about. So I suppose to a outsider we must be really looking like if we doing business and not God work. But it had to be God work, because them same years when Trinidad and Tobago was bawling for hunger was the very years when we make most a we greatest strides. I remember a song from that time that Tiger did sing. It go:

Time so hard you can't deny
In the forties saltfish or rice I can't buy
This war with England and Germany
Means only starvation and misery
But I going and plant and fix my affairs
And them white people could fight for a thousand years.

But we shoulda worry more about how we had was to fight down one another, than about the white people and their fight. Because Narayan, who is the man who was the editor a *The Hindu*, wasn't wrong when he make he little bird say what it saying, but he wasn't right neither. And a good bit a we story after that is about how that little bird was really a big ugly corbeau and how we had to find a stick to shoo it away from we. Ganesh was strong enough to do that, but the children a that big black corbeau still flying and sniffing all over this land.

112

CHAPTER 6: THE HINDU CORBEAU AND THE BIG GURU STICK

So much thing did start happening in the 1940s in that village because of we, eh! The village get electricity and standpipe. They even lay down lines so that people who coulda afford it get water straight inside their house. We get a proper road and we was able to build a nice house with a nice mandir that fit we new status in society. And biggest thing of all, we get telephone. We never thought it woulda reach Fuente Grove so fast.

Is just thirty-five miles from Port of Spain to San Fernando but things used to take forever to reach Sando, and then it had a way a stopping right there. Telephone reach Sando in 1940 so we thought we woulda have a long wait, but as I tell Ganesh, anything that coming south now, coming straight to Fuente Grove, because the most famous man who stay in south is he. He drawing everything he want straight to heself.

After that, Ganesh also do all the legal work to establish what he did call the Trinidad and Tobago Institution of Indian Culture. He did get to be a real boss about legal matters after he take away the case against Kaka from Randolph Nath and Sons and went to see Lawyer Kapildev about it. Just so he say it, eh, 'Lawyer Kapildev', like if is the man name. That happen soon after the case with the black cloud that he solve. Just so, one day he tell me that he fed up with how this case not coming to no conclusion and he hearing about this fella who now come back to Trinidad to practise, and people done start to talk about him and he going and see him.

He take the documents what Kaka did bring after we wedding, what Nath and them did give back to he long time, and he went Port of Spain to see this Kapildev fella. When Kapildev see the papers, Ganesh say he just shake he head sadly and say, "Is what

113

Raurav them fellas go suffer in, boy, when they cheating people so? This document that your Kaka hand you say that is he duty to hold all the property in trust. That just mean that if your Bap did dead while you was still underage, he younger brother woulda have to take care of the property until such time as you come of age to take care of it for yourself. Nath and them was fooling you into thinking that you have to keep on retaining them to keep your Kaka away from occupying the property. After the first time you went to see them they shoulda send a letter to him, explaining that his claim is absurd. And then they woulda have no further work to do. You never wonder why your Kaka never come back? You never wonder why the oil rights money keep on going into your account? You keep on paying them for nothing. I will write them up and make sure they get debarred."

Well, I don't know if is for gratitude, relief or shame that these people did take advantage a him for so long, and this man take away that burden, or what, but Ganesh do something he never do before. He invite this fella to come and visit we. He alone come one day and then he come back plenty other time with this or that friend and family and the two a them used to call one another on the phone and talk and thing – something like how Ganesh and Beharry used to be in the early days.

But it don't have plenty people like my Ganesh in this world eh! People start saying all kinda thing about how we house have more than a hundred windows and it have law that only the Governor house could have so much. They was saying how the man who build the roof for the house and mandir thief the timber from a estate in Carapal Village in Erin. All kinda thing they was saying. Some people does be so jealous of any progress another person making. Thank God that man Kapildev was we friend by that time and he tell Ganesh not to worry because all a them talking schupidness.

People did even get vex when Ganesh had to charge a entrance price for people to visit the very nice mandir that he get experts from India to design and build. It eh have nothing that people wasn't saying about we, up to how I dressing and where I going shopping and what we buying. Everybody in Trinidad know what kinda toilet paper Ganesh buy and about the two drawings of

Krishen Bhagwan what make with ink from the squid fish what Ganesh did put up in the drawing room.

Narayan was the man driving all these troubles that start landing on we head from this gossip. Most people can't do nothing to prevent anybody else from being happy, but in Narayan case, he pen could take away other people happiness and he put it to work with a vengeance. Phua was right to come and see we about what was going on with that little bird, as he used to call he self, because he coulda mash we up forever. That is why Ganesh had to pull out he pen, too, to counter that. And that is when Ganesh Publishing Company prove to be a very useful thing to have.

Ganesh work night and day to write a new book he call *The Guide to Trinidad* and he use the company to print it in. I see with my own eye how it start up. One day, he come home with a old old book name *Guide to Trinidad: A Hand-Book for the Use of Tourists and Visitors* by one James Henry Collens that print since Baba was a baby. And like that book give him a inspiration. Afterwards, everybody talk about that book as a masterpiece, but is Beharry who first discover why it was really good. Beharry, God rest he soul, did always remain the one person that reading anything Ganesh write and listening to everything Ganesh say very very carefully. When he read that book he say, "Allyuh wouldn't believe, until you done read the whole thing, how good this book is that Pandit write. He warn visitors to this country that even though the Carnival, the Phagwa and the Hosay could fool you, visitors should be very careful about jumping to quick conclusions. He say, 'Trinbagonians' – that is the word the Pandit use, you know, and I like it. He say, 'Trinbagonians are deeply religious and they are generally very straight-laced, so please do not think that some young man or woman would be willing to become romantically involved with foreigners.' He say, 'Come and look and enjoy but do not think that you can take what you see.' So I was just there enjoying how the pandit describing Trinidad and the wonderful landscape and interesting history, the extraordinary – them is the words he using in the book you know – mix of races that comprise its population. Then bam, he come to the interesting newspapers that start coming out and kill Narayan monthly in one shot. Pandit say to beware of these unscrupulous news media that are below standard and threaten to ruin the high regard of Trinidad in the international arena because of their disrespect for the truth."

"Well," Beharry say, "I don't think Narayan will get over that one no time soon. And the best part about it is that no one will ever know that is panditji who write it because that book eh have no author. Is anonymous. So that is it. Narayan done there for good, I feel."

When Beharry done talk, Ganesh say, "I didn't write it with Narayan in mind. I write it to expand the little world in which we living. I want you, Beharry, to make sure your shop have enough wine, whiskey, rum, Coca-Cola, soda and beer for big men and women and big drinkers. Yes, you hear me right, wine and whiskey included. And I want you, Leela, to make sure that all we cutlery matching and I want you to throw way them plates and cups that have little chip and thing on the edge. In fact, the best plan is that you should go San Fernando and get a set a matching tablecloth and matching napkin for all the tables and buy a whole new set a wares."

We get more than a little confused because it did seem like if all a we not talking about the same thing at all, at all. But by that time none a we not disobeying Ganesh, no matter how little the observation is that he might just make in passing. And this time is only when the army lorries and vans start pouring into Fuente Grove, I realise what them instructions was about. I realise that Ganesh did listening to me after all and did find a champion way for we to get some a the dollars with the man who look like a lady on it.

Them Americans didn't come to Trinidad to fight no just war, which is what they did saying. They was happy to come to Trinidad and Tobago instead a going Europe and they was here to sightsee and have a good time in the wild and wonderful West Indies, and they had plenty extra greenbacks, which is how them used to call their money, to throw around. Ganesh did send *The Guide* he write to all the army base to tell them what sights to see and he did write that Fuente Grove oriental temple, with its exquisitely carved elephants, gods and goddesses, was not a sight they could afford to miss. Many a them come with their Trinidad and Tobago girlfriends and even after they gone, word about who we was and what we look like get around the islands and far across the seas.

I used to feel proud when people call Ganesh my husband in them days, because I thinking that in one stroke Ganesh flatten Narayan like a cockroach under he shoe and same time he make heself more famous and plenty richer. And when you get big, well you big in true and Ganesh use that bigness like a stick to shoo away more corbeau like Narayan that feasting on the dead things in we communities. It didn't have nobody nowhere who didn't know Ganesh name and didn't think that Ganesh just like he namesake god. In them days, people in village like Fuente Grove still used to use the village panchayat sometimes to settle little quarrel and kuchoor case that the police and the Trinidad and Tobago court a law eh have no time to business with, or that people ain't satisfied about after the court done with it. Ganesh say one time that it was a very good idea that they doing that, otherwise things mighta get outta hand like how it happening with the steelband gangs.

Ganesh did start getting invitation from panchayat leaders all over the country to arbitrate the most difficult cases. He used to go quite up Princes Town, Tabaquite, Preysal, Phillipine, New Grant, Pepper Village, Rousillac, Piparo. Where in Trinidad Ganesh didn't have to go in them days doing that kinda work, boy? When Fyzabad Phua come to hear about it she did laugh and say, "Well look at that! This boy come out like me and inherit my work, the kinda work what I doing ever since your Poopha gone the other side." And she laugh so hard she couldn't catch she breath when Ganesh deliver a speech for she what he did make in one a them countryside place after he done deliver the decision a the panch. Ganesh perform he piece for she standing up on a chair in the kitchen. He say: "I would like to remind anybody here who would care to listen to the voice of good reason that County Victoria has the highest percent of library membership in the whole of Trinidad and Tobago, even though the population is only around 83,000 and we have the Carnegie Free Library in San Fernando to thank for that. In Port of Spain, although it have a population of 70,000, only about one percent is library subscribers. Here in south, we have the highest levels a literacy. The brains and the wealth a this country coming from the South."

Ganesh tell Phua that the crowd roar with pleasure when he say that.

But in all seriousness, going around to the panchayat meetings give Ganesh a chance to try to stamp out some a the nasty-mindedness that make people listen to rascals like Narayan. Word really start getting around about how good Ganesh does talk, and about the nice educational speeches he does make when he done and people start inviting we whenever they having Bhagwat or Ramayan, or Devi Yagya and sometimes even little satsangh and Maulood and Yeshu Katha. Whenever he talk in these kind a places, I remember he used to always start with, "Kitna Mahan Hai!! Bhagwan, Allah, Prabhu Yeshu Ki!!"

But before long, Ganesh did have to siddown and study about which invitation to accept. Because people used to real appreciate it when you go, and they treat we just like the pandit who sitting down on the singhasan or the imam or minister what leading their congregation. Many times the officiating pandit used to ask Ganesh to sit down next to him on the singhasan and to speak to the jajman from right there, and they used to put me to siddown in the front facening he. Just like how Ganesh used to work hard on he cases, so he used to work hard on what he going to tell people when he talking to them in this kinda gathering.

I didn't used to understand everything what Ganesh say, but sometimes he say things that I can't help but remember up to today. One time, when we went Coryal to a yagya, the pandit sing one song and make two words from that song he whole katha for the evening, and like that get Ganesh very annoyed. The two words was *bhav sagar* and the pandit keep on translating that as the worldly sea of life. Everybody was just nodding when the pandit saying how people should know that they not supposed to want anything from this worldly sea. The first thing come outta Ganesh mouth when he get up to talk was, "Bhav Sagar. What a beautiful phrase, man. Our poets sure do know how to express things correctly. Look at the wonderful phrase they have coined to describe the ocean of emotions in which all created things exist. What a wonderful thing it is to know how to navigate these emotions."

I don't know if anybody else realise that Ganesh make the pandit look like a arse, because nobody ever say nothing. But I never forget how easy Ganesh just get up and crush the man because he think the pandit talking schupidness.

But overall them days was good days, and that was when I finally lose my ganghri and orhni for good. I used to like to go with Ganesh. Other pandits didn't used to carry their wife with them or maybe their wife didn't used to want to go with them, but anywhere Ganesh going, he used to ask me if I want to come. I used to dress up in nice nice sari, what they did start selling in the Colours a India shop in San Fernando. I used to wear matching slippers, jewels and tika and we used to step out smelling and looking nice.

But, eh eh, as I say that, perfume is another interesting part of my adventurous life, you know. I used to smell good because Ganesh did buy a bottle of Chanel No 5 for we anniversary one time, when he did start to earn a little a he own money, and I did like that perfume so much that he buy it for me anytime I say that it running a little low. But it was me who did show him how nice it is to buy perfume and wear it and make it your own, by buying a bottle for he first and telling him every time he wear it how I smelling the Ganesh smell I love. And then he add he own piece to the ritual and start to kiss my neck whenever I wear the Chanel, telling me that I smelling like Leela Love.

But how this come to be a thing in we life is the interesting part a the story. It so happen that one day I went to F. W. Woolworth and Company in San Fernando and I notice that they have men perfume for testing. I went over to the counter to see this new thing that happening in Trinidad and Tobago, or maybe it wasn't a new thing but was just the first time I see it. The girl spray a perfume in the air to show me how they doing it and the smell nearly knock me down. It shock my system because Stewart ram goatie smell did still remain uppermost in my mind, but he must a used this perfume too, because I recognise the smell one time. I buy it and bring it home, but when I couldn't explain to myself why I buy it, I just put it in a drawer and I leave it there.

And then one day when we was getting dressed to go to a maulood, I see it when I open the drawer to get my wedding set to put on, the same one what Fyzabad Phua did put around my neck when Ganesh and he family come to arrange wedding right after Baba dead. I take it out and carry it in Ganesh room where he was dressing, and I tell him is a special present I get for him.

It did name Colony. I spray it on for him like how the girl show me. And that was that – the beginning of we perfume-wearing outside a the puja kinda perfume that we did accustom to. When we going to any a this kinda occasion, me and he used to step out looking and smelling nice and rich.

The only thing I didn't like from that time is that Ganesh used to object to sitting down on the singhasan when the pandit was playing harmonium, and up to now I don't know why he used to do that because I did like the harmonium-playing very much. It make the pandits look very nice and accomplished when they looking down at their book on the rayhal in front a them and singing while they playing the harmonium at the side a their body without looking at it at all. Then they used to stop and look up and explain what they did singing.

Sometimes we used to go yagya where a whole group was playing and singing and I did like those most. The harmonium, dholak and dhantal was something that did join all a we together as one, because whether you going Maulood or Yeshu Katha or whatever, very often was the same people playing in all. I mean is true that somebody might a find that if is the Hosein family, they might a sing the qawali with a little more feeling than the Yankaran family or the Dindial one and that Yankaran and them might do thumri better than the others, but is them same families, never mind who saying one better than the other, what singing the same songs all about. I used to think that them must a bring their harmonium and thing with them on the boat, and the younger ones born knowing how to play them before they could even walk and talk.

Even though we did have the fleet a taxi, at that time we did buy we first and last personal car. Was a Jaguar 2.5L Saloon. You must a see it when you was coming in because it still park up under the house and I does use it whenever I have to go anywhere. But when we did buy it, even though Ganesh willing to buy the car, it look like he didn't want to learn to drive it for some reason that he wouldn't tell me. So then I ask him if I could learn. He say no. He never tell me no for anything before, so I insist that he give me a explanation. He say it have plenty legal matters about getting a license to drive and he ain't have the time to see about that for either one a we right now. So, for any run we wanted to make, we used to hire one or two fellas as we driver who living nearby and working for we or for Beharry.

It did have a young fella name Jonathan who used to drive for we sometimes, and one day I just start following a idea that come to my mind. I explain to Jonathan that I don't want Mr Ganesh or anybody else to know, but I want him to teach me how to drive the car. He agree with no fuss, didn't even blink self when I ask, and he used to give me a few lessons, on the back roads, whenever he carrying me alone. And whenever I had to go somewhere close, like by Mildred or something, if Ganesh not home, I used to drive the car myself without asking anybody to go with me. If he home, I used to call for Jonathan and still drive for myself. On them days when we going yagya and other special occasions in we brand new motor car, whoever was the driver used to hold the door open for we just like they used to hold the door open all them years ago for Soomintra Didi when she visit we in Four Ways. I used to feel very happy and proud.

But some people is cockroach in true and Narayan didn't stay dead for long. Once he could crawl he start to attack we again. He papers did lose advertisers and income and for a while he didn't have much to say, but then he crawl outta the crack in the ground that he did gone to hide in, and he start up a whole set a new trouble for we. When Fyzabad Phua come to bring the news about Narayan attacks in town, Ganesh say one time, "Ah Marx against religion. Is a old card he drawing. I hear about this a long time ago from Indarsingh when I was still a boy. He wouldn't get far with that. The West Indies is not Europe and we believe in God and the men and women a God around here, even though we want the same kinda society Marx want."

I will never forget, too, that it was Beharry who realise Narayan true intention. That was in 1944.

Beharry say, "I go tell allyuh what that man up to. Next two years is election year, and if all the negotiating work out, it go be the first time this country have election what everybody could take part in, and that man gearing up to run for a seat." Everybody turn round to he because like all a we realise, same time, a truth that you can't argue with. Ganesh nod he head and say, "Is that self

I thinking." Then Ganesh say: "Is weeks now I watching *The Hindu* and how they start putting Hindu in front a any and everything – Hindu food, Hindu people, Hindu lifestyle, Hindu speech. And when you read what they write, you noticing that they not saying anything at all about real thing in real people life. The newspaper by-line is: '*The Hindu* is an Organ of Progress. I may not agree with what you say but I will fight to the death to defend your right to say it.' Clearly, they mean even if you ain't have nothing to say and all that you talking is schupidness. They talking about 'A Fair Day's Pay for a Fair Day's Work', and 'Homes for the Destitute' but we don't know who any a this referring to. A fair day's pay for who? Who is the destitute? Is the fellas who still cutting cane in the estate who does have use for these papers only in the latrine? When they want money, the homes suddenly get ownership and we hearing about 'The Hindu Homes for Destitutes Fund'. I seeing what they up to good good."

Fyzabad Phua tell Ganesh, "Well you better watch it. He eh attacking you in he columns right now, but he copying you in everything you do, in the way you talk, the way you walk, the things you saying and doing. And a person who doing that is a bigger danger than the person who attacking. Because if people start mixing up the two of you, and thinking he doing what you doing or you doing what he doing, then your dogs' dead."

She was always the one with she nose to the ground eh, even though she holding she head high in the air all the time, and is she who realise how me and Suruj Mooma could help Ganesh beat Narayan at he own kinda game and make sure at the same time that nobody could ever mix up the two a them. You see Narayan wasn't a marrid man and that does always be a drawback in politics I hear them say. So Phua tell we how we must do social work in the community like how all the proper modern housewives in San Fernando and Port of Spain doing them thing in they husband name. She say, "It simple. You just get some children together, bring them inside the restaurant, and feed them up. Or you go outside, look for children, and feed them outside. Christmas-time come round now, you pick up two three balloons and a few toys and you go round giving them away." It was a master plan and we start to do it once a week.

Word get around about the amount a good work the Social Work Committee a the Trinidad and Tobago Institution a Indian Culture doing for the poor people and the children a this country, while others spending their time trying to get as much as they can from others. In no time at all, people did coming by we to give their donations and take their picture shaking one a we hand in front the mandir. Even though we start it up to get at Narayan, we end up doing plenty good work, because from all my walking about the place I did come to know where it really had people who need help.

In the meantime, the more agitated *The Hindu* getting, the more Ganesh getting calmer and more collected. He reading and writing quiet quiet everyday, just like he doing since we come to Fuente Grove. I didn't use to have to carry out the cows no more by that time, although I used to still go and kiss DeviDoy whenever I had a chance early in the morning. We did have enough money to hire some fellas to take care a the cows and a few ladies from the village used to see about the milk.

All Beharry children was still in school that time and because government start a bus service for the school children, Beharry Bhowjie didn't use to have to worry about how they going and coming, not even about Suruj who did start to go Naparima College in San Fernando, so she did have more time and she start to hire people to cash in the grocery and in the bar and she used to come over to help me out in the restaurant and with the social work and all the other things I was doing. She and me was the only members a the Social Work Committee when we start, but plenty other people volunteer after.

A lady name Roma Mc Neal, who was the wife a the estate manager, and Tara Bidassie is two a them I does remember up to now, because once they start they stick with it and continue even after I leave Fuente Grove and Mrs Kapildev take my place. Just before I leave, the Colonial Secretary heself did write to say that he don't have the words to give a adequate picture of the really worthwhile efforts community groups like we one was doing, and he say that what even more impressive to he was that what we doing didn't owe nothing to no official textbook or model that somebody else make. I was thinking that is Phua model, but I don't suppose he would a think so. But what I trying to say is that it seem to me that because a what government doing, it had some people who coulda move outta the cane field and housework and find a bigger world out here, just like Ganesh and Beharry and me and Bhowjie. The ladies who could take work outside start to make the dahee now, and the dahee bara and lassi for the restaurant and all, and once a month they used to make the gheew we used to cook the meethai we serving in the restaurant and the meethai and prasad what Ganesh used in some a the pujas he doing for people. We did have to give up the coconut oil project because it was too much work for the handful a we, and I was sorry about that because food cooked in fresh homemake coconut oil don't taste like no other food you ever eat. That cause me to start back making my own oil to cook with after I come back here, because I did miss that while I was in town. But in them days, I did think that is only so much one person could do. But you know, other than them few changes, the pattern a life from when we did first come to Fuente Grove continue right through the years, even down to sewing one or two dress, kurta, choli and pants from time to time, and curtains, bedsheet and pillowcase every Christmas. But even that too did change soon enough, although I didn't know that was going to happen then.

I was content in them days and Ganesh stop telling me santosh na ba. I was still getting up early, but now I checking that everything in the restaurant ready for the workers to start breakfast and prepare the things for lunch. Then I making sure Ganesh things to bathe and he clothes ready for him. Those days we had hot water in the shower and somebody coming in to do the ironing, so I didn't have them things to do again. When Ganesh done do he morning puja I still used to serve him he breakfast first like always, before I go in the restaurant to take up work for the day. While I gone, Ganesh reading and writing. It looking to me like he ain't taking on Narayan at all. Instead, he studying about how plenty people did come to him to cure a problem we don't understand because we did never have it we self, and that is what he was writing about.

That problem was constipation. Ganesh did think a good bit about what people should do to prevent it and how to treat it if they have it, and the book that he write about it was the only book he write that I read from cover to cover. Look it here – the masterpiece that he call *Profitable Evacuation* and it had very profitable outcomes for all a we. What he do in that book was just remind people that they must drink enough water, but never with their food; that they must do exercise even if only it mean they planting up they kitchen garden like he wife does do; they must eat fresh foods what they pick straight from where it growing, if that is possible; and they must prepare and drink dahee regular. And like he used to watch what I doing to make it because he describe the process so good that I coulda just give the book to the ladies who coming to help we for them to follow if I didn't done teach them how to do it already. He describe many other common sense remedies like that, what I agree with totally. While I reading the book, I thinking is a strange world we living in for true if people don't know what to eat and how to eat and when to drink and what to drink, and their body don't know how to get rid of the rubbish they putting in it. But like that is the kind a world we living in, in this Kaliyug.

But while Ganesh minding he own business and attending to he client needs and writing good books, Narayan playing the arse because he want to get power of a different kind, in a different way and for different reasons, but he aiming he guns at Ganesh to get he different business done. I sure Ganesh woulda just continue to ignore him, but like it did eating up Beharry, and although he frighten to bring it up with Ganesh, he couldn't resist. Ganesh say he see too much election since 1925 and he see how electioneering was corrupting and he didn't want nothing to do with it. The way he was behaving didn't surprise me, because it was just like how Baba used to say so long ago, that he didn't want to get involved with the set a organisation they did forming up all over the country.

Ganesh describe people who does take part in election as "little children playing dolly-house and stick-em-up. The girls does finally get the boys to live with them in their dolly-house and the boys does get to be called the man a the house by robbing anybody that give them even half a chance, so that they could maintain the house. And Narayan party, that they call The Hindu Association, was a good example," he say, "of that very thing."

It had so much thing about that group that Ganesh didn't like. In that party first general meeting, every single member get a position. Narayan was President and it also had four Assistant-Presidents, two Vice-Presidents, four Assistant Vice-Presidents; many Treasurers, one Secretary-in-Chief, six Secretaries, twelve Assistant-Secretaries. People woulda feel hurt nah if somebody did remain without a position and it woulda be trouble for everybody if anybody did start feeling so. It had forty people in the association and every man jack had to have special perks to perform.

That is how this politics game was going on all over Trinidad and Tobago in them days and it only get worse in every other election I live to see so far. If I remembering correct, I think that in that 1946 elections it had forty-two candidates for just nine seats and it had five parties: The British Empire Workers and Home Rule Party, The Trinidad Labour Party, The Trades Union Council and Socialist Party, The People's Democratic Party, and The United Front. And then you had the other half a the country what didn't want to have nothing to do with them and their dotishess. On top a that, when the votes do count for that election, The United Front win three seats and the set a independents win only one, although they had more votes than any other parties put together. I don't think that things change much from them days to now. I remember how Ganesh laugh when he read in the papers that the Supervisor a Elections say how, "the people of Trinidad will be making up their bed for a long rest over the next five years. It is up to them to ensure how comfortably they will lie." Ganesh was so sure he didn't want to be involved in that kinda thing at all and woulda never be doing anything connected to politics. I suppose we was young and schupid then and didn't realise that everything was politics.

But if Beharry and Fyzabad Phua couldn't resist showing him what Narayan was doing, to try to push Ganesh to get into the politicking, what Ganesh couldn't resist was the group a people Beharry and Phua organise to convince him that he had to stand up against Narayan. And that is how a kind a politicking enter we life and start to change everything for good. Like everything else, it start slow slow and we couldn't make out then where it woulda eventually reach. Was just three men Phua and Beharry did send, one name Swami, who used to work for a solicitor quite up in Couva, one who Ganesh used to call in private, Post Office Partap, and a boy who respectfully call Partap, uncle, who also call Swami, Mausa, because Swami was he mother brother. He call Ganesh sir and Ganesh was impressed by the boy. I figure it was for two main things: first because the boy did get a first grade in the Cambridge School Certificate and, second, because he did find the idea a bringing out he own newspaper, what the boy was suggesting, very appealing.

But Ganesh is Ganesh and he didn't act on any a he feelings right away. What make him get up was the excitement that a fella did try to create with some fake news that he put out. I did feel that the journalist do that just because everybody was kinda fed up with the quietness all around the world when the war done, though same time people was getting very excited about Mahatma Gandhi and other business in Indian politics. But I learn much later that I was very wrong. People was afraid and that is why it was so quiet. Ganesh, on the other hand, simply react because he didn't like the fact that Narayan end up looking like a person a importance in the fake news. I remember seeing how Ganesh lips start moving over the words when he reading about Narayan in the papers. I does do that when I trying to sound out some words I never see before, but I never once see Ganesh do that until that day.

I keep that page what Ganesh read from in my folder. He read it out loud for me: "Chain-smoking, balding C. S. Narayan, veteran journalist, President of the extremist Hindu Association and leader of the Indian community in Trinidad and Tobago, received me at his party headquarters yesterday. Unlike Indian politics in which Gandhi's voice is a voice of peace, truth and non-violence, in Trinidad and Tobago politics there is no position to counter Narayan's." Ganesh get up when he done read it and start shaking up the papers saying, "But who is this Gadaha who write this schupidness about Narayan. What leader? What Indian community? You eh see Hitler shoulda really bomb way England arse if it so full of schupid people like this." I take the papers from him but I didn't understand right away what bothering he so much and I say, "But how you mean, man. The fella just describe how he meet Narayan and he saying how he one seeing what Narayan could mean to the future a Indians in Trinidad and Tobago." But Ganesh give me such a cut eye, I just turn and walk away because he was looking like he ready to do some violence. The only part of what he say that I understand was the part about Hitler bombing England when I realise that the writer a the article was a Englishman.

When Beharry come over, Ganesh start up again and it look like Beharry understand what going on better than me. When they done talk, Ganesh do something that I didn't see him do in a while. He get up and walk with Beharry to the door when he leaving that day, and I hear him saying, "I go do for Narayan. Just wait and see." Beharry, sounding happy happy, reply, "That is how I like to hear you talk, Pandit." Ganesh hit him on he back over and over and say, "Something bound to happen, Beharry boy. Something bound to happen and then you go see action."

It didn't take more than a few days before the thing happen. Fyzabad Phua come and the first thing she say as she put down she things and siddown in the drawing room was, "'Ah, boy, this Trinidad. What a place is this Trinidad." Ganesh say, "Yes Phua, all a we know is a hell of a place. But what make you feel so suddenly sad for it." She say, "Don't tell me all you ain't know what happening these days. You didn't see how much people getting their picture in the papers for giving donation to the Hindu Destitute Home Fund. Well, I hearing that all the money they give, Narayan taking and buying up estate cheap cheap from people who frighten by the talk that is internal self-rule now, but soon we going to start to talk about independence coming, too. These people selling up and going wherever they have friends and family living – in England, America, Canada. One or two family I hear even gone to Germany. Is not no Estates for Destitute Hindus that Narayan buying you know. Is for he self he buying them. And you know what the trouble is? He going to get away with it too! When people give money, you think they care who get it? Once they open they mouth and skin their teeth for a photo in the papers, they happy, you hear. And too besides, you believe they go want this thing to come out now for people to start laughing at them?"

Ganesh grab the chair behind him and ease he self down in it slow slow, and he saying, "Is like that nightmare with Kaka for my wedding all over again. What make Indian people so greedy and land hungry. What? What?"

"The question that eh have no answer," Phua say, "is why they have no sense a character and values and eh shame to be making all a we shame so? You have to get up and do something now, Ganeshwa. You can't let this go so."

Beharry come over same time because that is how Beharry was. It was like he used to be watching by we house and any sign a anything happening and he used to come over one time. When he reach, he have some news too. He say, "I hear that Narayan playing double role now. When he with Indian people he saying he is Chandra Shekar Narayan and when he with other people he is Cyrus Stephen Narayan. But some other people saying that he get the Narayan only when he reach Trinidad and Tobago. That he was Cyrus Stephen in Grenada where he born and grow up. That he only come to Trinidad and Tobago as a big man and now he settle down in we country and feel he could do whatever he please he mind to do. Pandit, I saying we shouldn't put up with that kinda schupidness from no foreigner."

It didn't take much to convince Ganesh after that and he just stand up as though he making a speech to a crowd and declare: "Send Swami and Friends back here. Let we make plans to put Narayan in he place. After the 1857 war, Queen Victoria declared to the world that no Indian subject shall be molested or disquieted, by reason of their religious faith or observances, but now it look like, after almost a century, Narayan trying to change that right now in front a we eye – like he plan is to finish what the plantation start against all the good intentions a the queen. We go have to launch we own newspapers to do for he."

CHAPTER 7: GANESH THE NEWS MOGUL

Must have been 1945 when Ganesh, Post Office Partap, Swami Mausa and the boy take over my dining room table and I lose it for good, because by the time they finish what they doing, it was time to leave Fuente Grove. The papers they design was very nice. The masthead was a picture a Mahatma Gandhi that Swami get somebody to thief for him from the *Sentinel* office. Underneath the picture they put Gandhiji words as their motto: *Satyagraha and Ahimsa*.

But the team didn't get along too good from the first day they start to work on the project because they was so different from one another nah. I try to make things nice for them by sending in a tray with some glasses a Coke on ice for them. You woulda think that that woulda make them a little more civilised, make them realise that they have common purpose, so they better overcome their differences. But from the start was plenty plenty trouble. The little boy with the first-class certificate, who everybody was calling Boy but who real name was Vyasa, object to everything and I see that maybe that is why Ganesh like him. He had something like a younger Ganesh about him and I was remembering how Pa and Ganesh does clash just like that but they still like each other and they have plenty a the same qualities and that is what does cause the clashing.

Boy say he don't like it when they say the papers will have four section. He say he don't like how they planning to attack under the words and picture of a man who stand for non-violence. He didn't think the three others woulda be able to full up the three other sections after Ganesh say he going to attack Narayan on the front page and put a report on my social work on the next page. The boy object to the next page when the rest say it will be the page a culture and advertisements. But when things look like they going to really heat up and somebody go clout him behind the head, he come up with a first class idea, that after culture should be film reviews and advertisements for film. And everybody say they like how he thinking.

But right after that, a fight nearly break out when Swami Mausa forget he self, because like he did get tired by the time they get to last page, and he bawl at Partap – something about if he lose he brains after working so long in the post office. I was sure Partap woulda mash up my good good glass on Swami head when he say that. Partap get up for him, saying, "Who does work in the Post Office? You could ever see a man like me licking stamps? You is the damn tout who does run around licking." Is a good thing I did paying close attention to what going on and get in there and take away the glasses from the table and the one in he hand and carry them go in the kitchen. You know is such a big insult to tell anybody that they licking, kissing or sucking up anything in this country, even up to now, eh. I suppose is because everybody does have to do it at some point in their life if they going to survive. I was sure Swami, who was the size a everybody else in the room put together, woulda lick Partap down with one blow, and the next thing you know somebody woulda be singing a song about what going on in my house.

But thank God, Swami check he self, one time. Swami say quick quick, "I did only making joke, man. Who could look at a man like you and say that you working in the Post Office? I could just look at you and see that you is a Parcel Post man. Parcel Post print all over you, man. Not so, Boy?" And like the boy sorry that things did start to go wrong, so he agree quick too. "He look to me like a Parcel Post man, for sure," he say. I step in at that point when I sure no blows will pass and tell them that they will have to get outta my house if they can't behave like decent people. But all a them start to say they sorry so fast, I couldn't even make out the sorry, but I know what they trying to say so I let them continue. Afterwards, I ask Ganesh why they does laugh at Partap for working in the post office. He say he feel is because a the set a laws that regulate every little thing that does happen in the post office, and like that does make people working there cokey blind with confusion and so slow it does look like if they come to a complete stop. I didn't really understand that so I just let it go.

After the little fight, everybody turn back to the last section and this time it was easy for all four a them to agree that it should really be a serious religious feature. But when it come back after that to a good name for the paper, which was the final item on the agenda, I did think they might a go at it again. Partap ask, "What about *The Sanatanist*, because it close enough to *The Hindu* but it emphasising we position on this Hindu business?" And then I finally understand what make the boy so objecting-able. He say, "I can't have anything to do with that. My father is a Arya Samajist." I think to myself one time, "Eh-heh. So that is why he so." He try to back back after that by saying, "Is also easy to twist that name to make it *The Satanist*." But I think by that time everybody did understand where he coming from and later I hear Ganesh telling Beharry that fellas like Swami should be more careful about who they involving in their business because these days the place full a Hari who is really Harry and Mariamma who is really Mary Ann.

But, if anybody did ask my opinion, I woulda tell them that the boy turn out to be alright after all. The young can only behave like the young. And was he self what come up with a very strong name for the newspapers. It was *The Dharam* and in a way it was like a apology to everybody to show that he know that the group form up to give voice to plenty people who thinking a certain way, and that what they trying to do is to insist that they believe in Sanatan Dharam and don't want people to think about them as Narayan kinda Hindu. When the boy suggest the name, he say, "Is a good way a showing Narayan and them that everybody can see through the fact that they trying to invent a people what name Hindu, when it really only have many many different people who trying to carry out their dharam as best as each person understand it, to the best of each person ability." Everybody clap for him when he say that.

As usual when Indian people get together to form a association it does always have a little kuchoor about position, but with only four a them and Ganesh not really interested in position, the matter settle easy easy. Swami name he self Editor-in-Chief and he say Boy will be the Sub-Editor. Partap was feature writer and compiler.

Ganesh accept it when they say he should be Business Manager and they accept it when he say that Miss Mildred sewing business and Beharry's Emporium, which was the new name Beharry give he whole conglomerate – what now make up a Surujdeo Grocers, Baldeo Magic Fountain, The Mahatma Sportsworld, Beharry Puja Shop and Gandhiji Touring Company, will be the main business what the papers going to advertise for.

But that was the easy part. Putting the plans into action didn't go so well. Even though Ganesh make sure that space reserve for Miss Mildred and Beharry business, them wasn't too willing to spend no money to advertise. Really and truly, Beharry didn't need no advertisement. Once people coming to see Ganesh, people seeing all Beharry business too, and plenty a them used to come back for just Beharry one alone.

Miss Mildred did have more work than she and she husband coulda handle even before I meet she, and them business did just keep growing. Mr Thomas was even talking about building a clothes factory in town because plenty more people did come to ask Miss Mildred to teach them to sew after she start to teach me, and when she reputation start growing, people used to send their children from very far to learn from she.

Lately, Miss Mildred did even start to contract out some a she work to some a them who invest in their own machine and who she trust. So even she didn't really need no advertising either. Even so, she and Mr Thomas get excited when I tell them about the paper, and is while I telling them that if we going to advertise the business, they have to give it a nice name that they come up with Martins' Fine Tailoring Establishment, which is what the many branches a their business from Port of Spain to Fuente Grove have up to today.

Getting other people to advertise was harder because the film distributors say they don't need nobody to review their film and they don't need to advertise in no fly-by-night papers because the better newspapers does done announce they film in town. In country, plenty people who going cinema can't read so announcement on radio and on the mic does work better for them. And that was true, eh. Still true up to today. People does just want other people to leave them in peace to enjoy their film. Nobody ain't want to read about what somebody else think about the film they went and see.

But the film review idea start up a very good part a my life for me, and up to now me and my friends does have a little movie date from time to time. That day me and Ganesh had we first one because he decide we still going to go to see a movie, not in Teelucksingh's Travelling Cinema what the Fuente Grove people does go to, but at The Palace in San Fernando. The boy went with we to see *Anmol Ghadi* and when he write he review, Ganesh give it the okay, and for the rest a the time Boy continue to write for the papers under Ganesh guidance. The next film we went to see was *Gilda*. But the one I did like best in all the ones we went to see together, and the boy write about, was *The Lady from Shanghai*.

When fulling up the pages with advertisement didn't work out, Ganesh hit upon a plan to put he favourite pieces from the writings a Mahatma Gandhi in the spaces instead and they put piece piece from all kinda thing that Gandhiji say on every page. And you know, I think that is like Ganesh did forget that in he first book is he self who try to develop a set a creed for Sanatanists to follow, and like all a them forgetting that we taking a stance against using the word Hindu to describe we. I still have a copy a that first paper. Look at where they put this in the middle column on the front page in the biggest type without thinking once self how it contradicting plenty thing they saying otherwise:

> It is the good fortune or the misfortune of Hinduism that it has no official creed. In order therefore to protect myself against any misunderstanding I have said Truth and Non-violence is my creed. If I were asked to define the Hindu creed I should simply say: search after Truth through non-violent means. A man may not believe even in God and still he may call himself a Hindu. Hinduism is a relentless pursuit after truth and if today it has become moribund, inactive, irresponsive to growth, it is because we are fatigued; and as soon as the fatigue is over, Hinduism will burst forth upon the world with a brilliance perhaps unknown before. Of course, therefore, Hinduism is the most tolerant of all religions. Its creed is all-embracing.
> Taken from *Young India*, 24 April 1924.

On the second page they put this one, and I was thinking that it would be a better idea for them to put that one on the first page, but when you dealing with a set a men, sometimes it don't be so easy to speak up. This one is where Gandhiji write:

I have ventured at several missionary meetings to tell English and American missionaries that if they could have refrained from 'telling' India about Christ and had merely lived the life enjoined upon them by the Sermon on the Mount, India instead of suspecting them would have appreciated their living in the midst of her children and directly profited by their presence. Holding this view, I can 'tell' American friends nothing about Hinduism by way of 'return.' I do not believe in people telling others of their faith, especially with a view to conversion. Faith does not admit of telling. It has to be lived and then it becomes self-propagating. Nor do I consider myself fit to interpret Hinduism except through my own life. And if I may not interpret Hinduism through my written word, I may not compare it with Christianity.
Excerpt from *Young India*, 20 October 1927

On this other page, where they did leave space for a next advertiser, they put this one:

It is clear that Hinduism is not an exclusive religion. In it there is room for the worship of all the prophets of the world. It is not a missionary religion in the ordinary sense of the term. It has no doubt absorbed many tribes in its fold, but this absorption has been of an evolutionary imperceptible character. Hinduism tells everyone to worship God according to his own faith or dharma, and so it lives at peace with all the religions.
Young India, 6 October 1921

You will notice that the length a the pieces they taking and the size a the print they choose did depend on how much space they did leave for the advertisement they thought would a go in that spot. The next one they take is this one:

I do not consider myself worthy to be mentioned in the same breath with the race of prophets. I am a humble seeker after truth. I am impatient to realise myself, to attain moksha in this

135

very existence. My national service is part of my training for freeing my soul from the bondage of flesh. Thus considered, my service may be regarded as purely selfish. I have no desire for the perishable kingdom of earth. I am striving for the Kingdom of Heaven which is *moksha*.

Taken from *Young India*, 3 April 1924

And on the last page they have this one under this big heading "The Greatest Readings of All":

About helpful readings, we have regular readings of the Bhagawadgita and we have now reached a stage when we finish the Gita every week by having readings of appointed chapters every morning. Then we have hymns from the various saints of India, and we therein include hymns from the Christian hymn-book. As Khansaheb is with us, we have readings from the Quran also. We believe in the equality of all religions.

Harijan, 5 December 1936

Every week they do the same thing and I think the one great good they achieve wasn't that they get people to stop reading *The Hindu* and start reading *The Dharam* and take away Narayan voice from him, it was that they educate the readers about Gandhiji, even me and all, and I think plenty a we was waiting for chances like this to get a education about who we is. I didn't keep all the papers. I just keep this one because my report, "The Fountain of Social Work" by Leela Ramsumair, did look very nice indeed. I could tell you that.

But watch at what my article have under it. This is how they used to full up all the rest a the papers until *The Dharam* stop coming out. The process was simple. Ganesh used to watch what going on in the other newspapers and he used to just copy over anything he see what he want he readers to know.

One morning he say, "You ain't seeing how suddenly every-body eye turning South, as though all the answers to all the problems a the nation lock away down here. Hear Kelshall, nah" and that is how come this piece here get in this papers:

We have here riches in soil and climate and most of all, riches in oil. These riches must be more equally distributed. We must see to it that the dividends these oilfields make year after year remain in this island to be spent by you, the people of Trinidad and Tobago. If we believe that they are not giving us a fair deal we can follow our brothers in Mexico and expropriate them or pay for them what we consider a fair price by giving Government bonds.

"Riches! Riches!" Ganesh say, "that is all they know to talk about." The next week he follow up on it and write this long article in *The Dharam* with a big headline "No Guarantee of Happiness in Material Possessions" to talk about why he don't agree with the idea that building a nation is about throwing people out. By that time they was grabbing the ball from Narayan and it was looking like it didn't have no come back for he. I didn't read the article, but I remember Swami and Friends and Beharry and all get very excited about it and they was saying that Ganesh sound like the Guru all a them know him to be.

Ganesh tell them: "Well it looking like allyuh ain't paying close enough attention to what allyuh Guru saying, because allyuh ain't see I tackle Solomon or what? Somebody had to respond to all they dotish talk about unity. Just bawling at people about unity all the time not going to make people united. It just showing how the people who in this politics business can't stop being like longtime overseers who will bring their whip down on your back if you don't do what they saying. And you notice how they like to talk in twos and threes, too eh. I feel they think the population can't count more than three. They talking about three-part project for change. It sounding good eh – change of government, change of ownership and nationalization of the country's industries and a change in stinking thinking through mass education – but I don't like the tone one little bit, so I had to tell them it sound like brain washing and daylight robbery. I had to remind them that robbers does hardly ever understand what they thief and does end up throwing it away because they don't know how to use it."

The fellas say, "Nah man, Pandit. How you could say so? We seeing that that is what you doing, Pandit."

And then it had one big issue that Ganesh pick up and never put down even when he wasn't writing in *The Dharam*. That was about how much a the people who did come from India still couldn't talk English, and that was a big problem that plenty people was concerned about. Ganesh start reporting on what different different fellas was saying about it. He write about how for the last election the members a the constitution reform committee did talk a lot about the language barrier and effective citizenship and then the government still went and make competence in the English language a condition for registration as a voter.

He say how Adrian Cola Rienzi was complaining that the language barrier disenfranchising one group a people in this country – the Indian illiterate in English. Ganesh say that Rienzi right to raise the issue and he tell everybody that they should sign a petition he put in the papers to show their support for Rienzi. He say that if the government continue with this discrimination, then Trinidad Indians have to alert the Secretary a State for the Colonies so that some safeguards could be put in place to protect we rights as a minority group.

But then, all this newspaper publishing business did end for Ganesh after about six months because a letter come from the Governor and the Governor chauffeur deliver it to Ganesh by hand. Everybody come out to see the car, even though it was a Jaguar just like we one and it wasn't as if they did never see we own before. They come out because everybody recognise the Governor car and they might be thinking that the Governor heself was coming to see we.

I don't even have the words to describe to you how proud Ganesh feel when that letter come quite down here to Fuente Grove to let him know that they would like to appoint him as a Member a the Legislative Council. He read out this line where the Governor write that "as a functionary of His Majesty, King George VI, he has been commanded to guide colonial peoples along the road to self-government within the framework of the British Empire. We would like to invite you to participate in this process with us and do hereby request a response from you about your willingness to be appointed as a Member of the Legislative Council in the swearing in ceremony for new members in 1946."

Ganesh keep on saying, "Watch at this. Watch at this. It even sign by His Excellency Capt. The Hon. Sir Bede Edmund Hugh Clifford."

Ganesh call up Kapildev right away and tell him what happen. He explain that he don't know what is the proper way to respond to the Governor letter. Kapildev say, "Man, that is a victory for Ranjit Kumar! You know how long he asking for more nominated members from among the common people." Then he tell Ganesh not to worry. He will take care a the letter for he and since he already in town he will deliver the letter heself to the Governor. After he done do that, Kapildev call back Ganesh the same day, but not only to tell him that he do as he promise, but to encourage him to come up to Port of Spain to live. Ganesh tell him that that really not possible because, even though he make some money over the years, he don't have enough to buy a house in town. Again, Kapildev say not to worry. He say he willing to buy the Miracle House and Mandir, which is how most people did come to refer to we place, and after that he could also see about buying a property in St Clair for we, close to where he family living. Ganesh agree and so my life in Fuente Grove come to a end, just like that, and I had to start to put things in place for we to move to the city.

CHAPTER 8: IN TERROR OF THE CITY

Going to town in time for the first sitting of the Legislative Council after the 1946 elections, which was the third time I move in my life, wasn't nothing like when we move to Fuente Grove, and while we driving to town I was remembering how Ganesh did put on a brave face that time and how he was talking non-stop whole road about how excited he feeling to start life in this new place with me.

This time, though, he did just sit down quiet in he corner, looking out the window. I myself wasn't feeling to talk too much, because I was feeling sad to leave Fuente Grove. When we was leaving I was thinking it was just a mood, but in truth it was like I giving up my whole life, that I was making a bigger sacrifice than I did think I was capable a doing. As it turn out, the mood did come to stay, because it was a whole nother life we did have in town, and even when things was bright and glittering, underneath it remain sad all the time.

The only time things brighten up a little bit inside the car self was when Ganesh catch a little story-telling soor. We was getting close to Claxton Bay and for some reason, Ganesh start to remember he father and it was like Baba come back to life for me in the way Ganesh start talking. Ganesh turn to me and he say, "You know, Bap just cross my mind in a funny kinda way. I remembering that first day when he was bringing me to school in town on the train. When we reach here so, he tell me the story of a dead girl who people does still see walking hurry hurry or running sometimes as if she late to go somewhere. They does see she all around this area here. Like she spirit can't let go of the duty she was trying to perform at the moment that she dead and it keeping on trying to fulfil it up to today. Bap say that she is the ghost a the white overseer daughter on the Forres Park Estate and she dead when I did just turn three years old in March that year and that is how he remember. She was only seventeen years old when she dead and it make anybody who hear about it sad. After it happen, though, some fools did start saying that was a cobra what did bite she, how the Forres Park Estate did bring in some indentured people from the last boat who does pujay karay snake, and when they was going in the boat to leave India they bring their God with them and it get away same time the girl was running and it bite she and she drop dead one time.

Bap tell me: 'I don't know nothing bout no cobra. But I know for sure that is snakebite she dead from, whether or not was a cobra. The girlchild did name Maria and it so happen that like all children, the children on this estate used to play together. And she and one a the little Indian boys name Indar who grow up together find that they can't do without one another, which is how this thing does always happen. Is so self it happen with your mai and me and is so self it will happen for you, although I could help out by checking the patra a the girls we know and telling you which one is most likely to be she, just like how my Bap do for me. But like that is not how Maria father and mother looking at it. Maria understand that very well, after they tell she that they want to send she away to get a good education because the governess they employ do as much as she could do for she for now. But Maria tell them that she love the boy Indar and she plan to get marrid to him and she not going away for no education unless Indar coming with she.'

"Like the parents was talking over this thing one day and she hear them planning to get somebody to kill Indar to get rid a the problem – that is how they calling she feelings. She take off from the house to tell Indar what they saying and she take the fastest track to reach the barracks where Indar living with the rest a he family. But it so happen that that is where they did just done make the fire trace around the canefields that they was going to burn the next day. Now, whenever you do that, all the creatures living in the field, especially the snake and scorpion, does run out and head for higher ground or for where it have water.

"Maria run up the hill, along the side a the river, a thing she

141

woulda know not to do if she used to pay enough attention to what happening on the estate. Something did bound to happen to she when she make that choice. It so happen that it was a snake that get she. The creatures does done be rile-up about the fire, and if the snake did just get what he think is a safe place for he and he wife, and then big ugly people foot start coming at them, insteada running away as he woulda normally do, he just fire bite instead. Maria keep on running, though, even after she get bite, because she must be feeling that she have to make sure that Indar know that she parents want him dead. Baychara, she must be thinking all kinda thing about how they could run away together and live happily ever after. By the time she reach the top a the hill, she was too weak from the effects a the snake poison and she fall from the top and break she neck. The men the father did send to get rid a Indar find she body."

I did never hear that story before and when I tell Ganesh so, he make the driver turn off the main road to show me where the parents build a statue on the top a the hill from where Maria fall to she death. I ask Ganesh what become of Indar. And he shock me when he say that he don't know, but if he was the boy who that did happen to, he woulda throw heself from the top a the hill to join she. But he don't think Indar do that, otherwise Maria ghost wouldn't a keep wandering all over the place looking for him still. As a matter of fact, Ganesh say, after all this time she probably don't even remember why she still running up and down. When we turn back for the main road, I move closer to Ganesh and put my head on he shoulder, and he lean he cheek down on top a my head. We mighta stay just so until we reach in town because that was a sad story and it make we feel sadder than before, but we stay so for a little while only, because he break the stillness and the silence inside the car for a second time for another story.

It happen just a few heartbeats after we just pass McBean Village in Couva. Ganesh tell the driver, "Humphrey, I want you to go a little slower after you come outta the McBean stretch. I want to show Mrs Ramsumair a house somewhere right after you pass Freeport Junction. But I can't remember exactly where it is." The driver say, "I will do that, sir. I think I know the house. Is the

MacLeod House after St Mary's Junction, not so? I know it good. Plenty people does want to stop there and just look at the house a little bit, and although the woman, Sita, still living there, I never hear anybody say that somebody ask to speak to she yet. Is almost as though everybody respect it as a holy story and all they want is to just stop and look at the house where this story come into being."

I get so excited to hear that it have another good story coming up that I cut their conversation short by saying, "Okay, okay. Tell me the story before we reach the house so I will know what to expect. Drive slow, Humphrey, so Mr Ramsumair could finish the story before we reach." And like Ganesh react to my excitement so he start up in a singsong way:

"Once upon a time, there was this young officer working in the British East India Regiment. His name was Norman McLeod. He was a good soldier who serve the empire well. When he had to retire on account of an injury, he didn't return to Scotland. Instead, he came to live in the plantation house that his father had built in Trinidad which the old man had called Bruadarach: Taigh na MacLeod na Dunvegan, leaving a little bit of his Scottishness behind before he left the overseer in charge and went back home.

"Now, unlike the father, what was interesting about Norman was that during his time in India he had come to believe in all the principles of Sanatan Dharam, perhaps even more than many of we who born and raise in them. When he come to this house and realise that many of the people on his estate believe as he did, he add a mandir to the house. He was already living there for many years, worshipping like them and with them, when one day he meet the daughter of one of the workers on the property. Her name was Sita."

Ganesh stop right there and I poke him and ask, "What you stop for?" He say, "Well, I was thinking that you might a know the rest. You can't guess?" So then I say, "He like she and they get marrid and still living there happily." He laugh at me then and say, "No. Is not so the story go. You go be disappointed, ent?" When I say "Just tell me nah, man," he finished the story off.

"They recognise each other alright, but Norman tell everybody that he knew immediately when he saw her that she is the

143

reincarnated soul of his dead mother and of course he has always treated her as such. It is, as Humphrey say, a holy love story, and Sita did live happily ever after, and they all live right there in the house I want you to see. Sita is one very fortunate woman. She must have done many good things in her last life to have reaped such a unique fate."

But after this storytelling, Ganesh became very quiet and I stay quiet too, because when we was getting ready to move to Port of Spain, I think about how much torture it was for Ganesh to go to school there and try to find a job there. I see how he used to get whenever he remember anything about them experiences, and the way he would only say one or two things make me see how much he don't want to remember.

He talk a lil bit easier about the two years he spend in the Government Teachers College, but like he didn't have no good years in Port of Spain at all except for the two in the Teachers College. And a good few a the fellas he used to know in them time did start to come by we to visit him when they start hearing about all the things he doing. Now, I understand, eh, that people used to end up in Teachers College in many ways. In the CM schools especially, once you finish primary and post-primary you could become a monitor and if after a few years they see that you could become a teacher, you would get to go to College. Soomintra Didi does complain up to now, in fact, that if Pa wasn't so schupid and did allow she to convert, she woulda get pick to be a monitor. But Ganesh didn't go to college that way. He get in with a second grade in the Cambridge School Certificate and because a that he woulda be like a boss in the place. But the other experiences definitely didn't look like they was good for Ganesh, at all at all.

Ganesh say that he did enjoy College because the Marriott-Mayhew Commission did cause the old curriculum to get throw out and new regulations come out for Primary Schools from 1935. He say he come first in class in teaching college because he believe so much in the philosophy a the new regulations. They insisted that each child is a different child and the teacher in front a the class have to take responsibility for the learning a each one a them. He say the scheme a work he design for he teaching practice pass round from hand to hand because he did make sure that every single lesson have enough activities for every child to be able meet the objectives set for the lesson. Everybody wanted to copy from it.

So, of course, when he tell me that, I did think that maybe the teaching job he did have after college would be a better experience than the rest for Ganesh. But he say that when he go in a real school is only to find that it didn't have no chance to do nothing like what he learn in college. The school they send him to was like a sheep farm and the teacher was just the dog that making sure the sheep keep in line. One time, he say, "Girl Leela, I couldn't handle the teaching job they put me to do at all. None a the teachers didn't use to teach in them schools it look like. Nothing that we learn in College was any use. In them schools it was a straight case a big man handling big man who just happen to be a little younger than them. It was the pummelling fist and the master's long stick at work to earn respect, never the gentle touch of persuasion they talk about in the books.

"When the headmaster sit down under that picture of George V and start preaching to me that I there to form not inform, and when I protest about what going on because I coulda see with my own eyes that it was really to deform not inform, I had to get the hell outta there. I run for my life and sometimes I feel like I keep on running and I eh stop yet. The headmaster say I lucky because they give me a position in town. But I feel that maybe if I did happen to get a position where it have children like Beharry one, maybe I mighta make it as a teacher. But not in town, boy. Not in town. In town, the schools was brutal.

Little by little, other pieces start to slip out as we packing up to leave. He tell me how Mrs Cooper laugh at he and Bap when they reach she house in Dundonald Street where Bap carry him to stay. He explain that by that time Kaka was done living in Laventille and when Mrs Cooper laugh at them, he wish Bap did carry him by Kaka instead. But Bap say it woulda be too far for him to walk to school and it didn't have no bus from there to the school. Ganesh tell me how when he try to make friends with another Indian boy name Indarsingh, he laugh at him too and call him a country bookie who father had to buy a place in the school for him to come there. Ganesh tell me how he did hate Bap for carrying him and leaving him there.

145

He try to explain to me how is a funny thing that does happen to you when you face other people hate or scorn, and it is that you don't want to push back their hate and scorn in their face. Instead you does start to feel like if you do something sometime, when you can't even self remember, and you deserve they hate and scorn. He say how he remember reading something about how in them days when Bap carry him to the town school, Indians were seen as a backward and violent group because in the Indian countryside there were many murders and all kinds a acts of violence, and this give the Trinidad Indians a fearful reputation. And he say how people like him and me, who know that all a that is not true, never tell nobody so, even though them kinda thing does affect you in so many ways, right inside a your own house because it affecting you in your mind and heart. You does stop knowing how to behave natural and does become afraid and distrusting about everything.

Ganesh say it take him a long time to understand how all this affect what Bap do when Bap sit him down after the janeo ceremony and tell him some of the family stories. He tell him Dada story about how Dada wife did move out when he hit she one time and when Dada went to bring she back, she say she not coming, that when is he and she alone, like he don't know how to control he rage, so is either he go back by heself or stay there by she mother and father house where she know somebody will kill him if he raise he hand against she again. Dada accept what she say and move in by them. Ganesh say it was stories like this and Bap's story about how Kaka take he whole family and move with them to Laventille, because he say that he fed-up with how we Indians backward in we way a thinking and living. Ganesh say that all that help him see why Bap take him to town and pay for he schooling. Ganesh tell me how he does feel so guilty about it now but at the time, all he could think about was things like the time Bap carry him back to school to face the shame a having a bald head, with a big churki leave back in the middle that them fellas used to take great pleasure in pulling. He realise later that Bap wanted him to be something big and up until now he didn't know how to do that, how he had been fighting up he whole life to make it worth he father effort, and he don't know if he will ever achieve that.

When he say that, I hug him up tight tight and tell him, "You don't know what you saying, man. Baba did love you more than he own life and you never had to achieve nothing to prove nothing to him. He only ever wanted you to be happy. You know how much years now I thinking that if Baba coulda see you, he would be so proud a you, Ganesh. How you could be thinking so? Look how Phua and all tell you how proud she is. Hush nah, man. Your father looking down on you right now and smiling at your foolishness."

He hug me back tight and we stay so for awhile and then he walk away and siddown and start back with he memories again. He tell me how he father give a lumpsum of $3600.00 to that school – five years worth a oil royalty – and then he turn around and pay $15.00 a term for him to go there for four whole years. Bap give them the same amount in prize money when Ganesh done pass the exams and still, still Ganesh always feel like he was never welcome there. He say he can't forget that those people don't have no respect for the effort that earning that money take. He tell me how people in the school used to think he and Indarsingh was friends because sometimes Indarsingh used to say, just so, 'Let us go for a walk in the Botanical Gardens,' in front a everybody, and true true country bookie that he was he used to agree. But Indarsingh only wanted company to practice he speeches and poetry and in less than a year after, he went to England and Ganesh never see him again until he start making the set a political noise we start to hear when he join Narayan and company.

Ganesh say that is only after he walk away from the school where they did send him to teach that he and Mrs Cooper start to become friends. It was as though she feel sorry for him because he was more like she than all the rest a the boys, and she used to stop and talk to him when all the young boys did gone to school and she see him siddown alone by heself. She even wrack she brains to think about another job when he leave the teaching work, but he say that is when he realise how much he didn't want to have nothing to do with what does go on in town.

Mrs Cooper tell him she have a cousin working in the Motor Vehicles Licensing Authority Office, and she go ask him if he could fix Ganesh up with a little end as a licensing officer. When

Ganesh tell she that he can't drive, she say, "Don't worry. You wouldn't have no driving to do. You just have to test other people driving. Is them what have to do the driving, and once they give you the money for their license, you just have to give them it."

Ganesh say he does frighten to think now about what kinda person he coulda turn into if Baba death didn't call him back to country.

CHAPTER 9: ADJUSTING TO THE CITY

But even though Ganesh make all that complaint before we reach in town, after we get to the house Kapildev did buy for we on Hayes Street and we settle down, it look like Ganesh set about becoming a part a the city with a great deal a energy. First step he take towards he goal was a change a clothes. I think that me and Beharry did do too much of a good job on he, and he remember the lesson too well about looking the part. It was back then that he ask me to tie he first paghri for him when he occupy the seat a the mystic for the first time. In town now, Ganesh begin to dress in three-piece suit with fat sailor pants that was in fashion back then, complete with a bow-tie when the occasion demand. He buy different hat to wear at different times and a set a shiny shoes in different shades a brown and black and khaki. He call them brogues sometimes and wingtips at other times. I don't know if them is different names for the same thing or different things or what. All a them did look alike to me. Mr Thomas was the one who help to fix him up with all that he need, and I not joking when I telling you is so Ganesh used to dress all all the time.

One time I try to tease him by asking him if he didn't notice how Trinidad Indian people start wearing kurta suit like Nehru. But he bark at me, "Well I prefer not to reach all the way over here in Trinidad and Tobago in the twentieth century, and then look like if I just walk out onto the stage here straight from the seventeenth century in India." On a very rare occasion, he used to put on a dhoti and sleeveless vest when he done bathe in the evening, and sometimes he used to fall asleep so and get up in the morning looking so. But it was a very once in a way kinda thing that only happen on them days that he set aside to read some books that he buy before we come to town and what he make sure was pack up and send up here even before we reach. Look at these books on the bookshelf here. Some a them come back down with me, like this one by C.L.R. James. *Life of Captain Cipriani: An Account of British Government in the West Indies.* But not this one here: Hewan Craig, *The Legislative Council of Trinidad and Tobago.* I remember when Ganesh buy that one. It was a few months before everything come to a end in Port of Spain for we.

After Ganesh leave, like I catch the book-eating sickness from him. I buy this one by Don Taylor, *The Years of Challenge: The Commonwealth and the British Empire, 1945-1958* and I buy this book here, Frank Hercules, *Where the Humming Bird Flies.* And look at what they write here in this book. To tell you the truth I don't think the writer was so wrong in this description he give a this party in Government House, you know:

> Among the guests was a number of black men, some of whom tended toward an uncompromising formality in their attire. They were dressed in the conventional English morning coat and striped trousers with top hat. One or two wore spats as well. In this way and in that scorching heat, they demonstrated the last full measure of their devotion to the Empire, their black chins notwithstanding, they were Englishmen, spiritual Englishmen and but for the incident of their birth on this tropical island and the accident of their ancestral derivation from Africa, they were as Saxon as Cedric and more royal than the true Richard.

My Ganesh wasn't from Africa but he mighta very well be looking exactly like one a the people in the party what they talking about in that description.

And it wasn't only on the outside that you could see this. Ganesh was excited for so after he come back from the first legislative council meeting he went to. He couldn't done telling me about how the governor talk about all the development works that the government doing. He explain to me that these works are broadly of two types. That is how he say it and I could see that he like the way they sorting the business they have to do. One type is about improving the social environments in which people live and the second is about producing revenue or increasing the economic assets a the Colony. The first type is all kinda thing like hospital, health centre, dispensary, school and other kinda training institution. He say they also looking at the housing for labourers, to make sure that they living in pleasant, healthy surroundings.

What what Ganesh didn't have to talk about that first day! He was so exited. He even call Beharry to tell him about it. He say that the Governor explain that the members will be asked to vote on these matters during their period of service on the Council. Then he talk about the high tension transmission line from Port of Spain to South that they thinking about, and how running that line and putting up all the electrical sub-stations will cost approximately $1,000,000. He say, "Leela girl, they spending that money to make sure that every household have electricity and that, down the road, businesses could set up anywhere, especially for the people in the oil business."

It was like when he write that first book. But now he thought he was finally doing something big and useful. He couldn't done talk about the island-wide water supply schemes for both Trinidad and Tobago that they done start with storage reservoirs in Caura and Hillsborough. He talk about how they had to relocate a whole village to do that. He tell we about the proper drainage and irrigation what they making plans for, so that our agriculture could feed the people in we own country, to prevent the kinda food shortage it did have during the war. He say, "This is a ten-year scheme you know, girl. Is not a little operation they talking about. It costing $500,000 to drain the Caroni Plain alone. Oropouche is next and it going to cost the same. We could afford to do that here because we done negotiate a ten-year rice agreement with British Guiana. They also going to be developing recreation facilities in Maracas and Tairico Bay and they planning to get rid a the swamp next to them to make the place healthier.

"Girl, they planning to make Piarco Airport plenty bigger, like international airports all over the world. You know how much they put aside for that? Five and a half million dollars. And they say that the British government done doing a great deal to make sure British West Indian Airways have everything it need to link up all the British Colonies in the Caribbean with one another and also with our foreign neighbours. They also planning to extend the Churchill-Roosevelt Highway but they not going to keep on draining the swamp and fulling it up downtown and going up Laventille side because they say DDT controlling malaria now.

"And girl Leela, we was making up we newspaper just so when it have a whole world a newsmaking and rules and regulations about broadcasting that we didn't know nothing about. The Governor say he now done negotiate for twenty hours a local broadcast on the BBC, and he waiting for further developments in the Empire Broadcasting Schemes. And Leela, all this time we quietly collecting we oil money, never knowing how much talk does have to talk to make that happen, and is the Colonial Office and the Ministry of Fuel and Power what in charge a all that. Leela girl, this government business is plenty work for true and it have more thing to do than I ever imagine. You know how much annual revenue them have to rake in to do all the thing they doing and they planning? $31,777,604.00."

I never forget them figures, just like I never forget the number a Vishnu car what he or he son must be still driving that time here in Four Ways. Vishnu come and dead a year after I come back here, and he son take he family and leave for Canada soon after; so I don't know what become a that car. But that don't have nothing to do with this.

I was explaining how I get a ringside seat to watch while Ganesh teach heself to like the fact that he end up back in the city, and started to believe that the city was the place to make a big contribution to the country through the work a the government. Sometimes it used to make me think how different he really was from Baba. When Ganesh start talking about the Carnegie library in Port of Spain, like if he never go in a library before in he life, I remembering how Baba didn't trust the banks, even though we didn't have no choice but to bank with them, and Baba used to do that in the full knowledge that he eh have no choice, and he just making the necessary concession until better could done. One day Ganesh say: "You know, Leela girl, we have to learn to talk about the international perspective on things. Look at how we've been benefitting from people like Andrew Carnegie's desire to promote the advancement of knowledge and understanding. It is because of the gifts of the Carnegie Corporation since November 1911, when you born, that people in this country have been able to get so many good books to read. I know that fellas like my friend Kapildev might remind me that the gifts were intended for libraries and church organs in Canada and in the United Kingdom, and only lastly in the British Colonies, but the point is that one must aim to be noble in one's desires to do the greatest good, and then only will one be living the good life. I have been hearing things like this since I was at QRC, but in my childish way I didn't pay attention when they were talking about that in school."

When he start to talk so, it make me remember how, even when we did first reach Fuente Grove, he was forever making pronouncements that I could never understand. Same now, except that since we reach in town he pick up pipe smoking. Sometimes it didn't used to have nothing in the pipe, but the pipe forever in he mouth and he used to take it out and put it back in and take it out and put it back in, a hundred times while he saying something. One time, he say, just so outta the blue, "The Compulsory Education Ordinance did pass since 1821, you know, but it was only for Port of Spain and St James – not for the whole country. That was during the time of Governor Sir Ralph James Woodford. And back then, before we Indians come, and long after we come, in fact, it was only Trinidad, and not Tobago. Tobago only get join up to Trinidad as a ward in 1899. Now, I have to warn you, Leela, that we have to start thinking about weself as Trinidad and Tobago, and sometimes I does notice that you does just say Trinidad when you talking. You must make the effort to say Trinidad and Tobago."

I remember another time when we take a drive down Chaguaramas and went for a walk along the shore. I was enjoying myself and was just about to ask him if we could do this more often, and if he think is alright for me to buy one a the bathing suits like what all the girls on the beach wearing, when he unbutton he jacket, put one hand in he pocket and take he pipe outta he mouth and start waving it at the sea, saying: "I suppose an important consideration, which would have led to the location of the earliest settlement on this side of the island, was no doubt the protected anchorage which can be found in these calm waters of the Gulf of Paria. The other coasts of Trinidad, as you know, are dangerous, owing to swirling currents and heavy breakers."

I didn't know what to say after something like that. I just thinking, "Well, I don't know no other coast, so how I go know if is true or not." And then it cross my mind that he ain't know no other coast either, except for the wharf down in San Fernando, where I never used to go because it always have some very iffy looking people down that side. I didn't know if that was what Ganesh was thinking about, but if it was, then he shoulda be able to see that he wrong, because it don't seem like the boats I used to see there did have any trouble anchoring. And then I think about Carli Bay where we turn off the main road to go and see the statue a Maria, and how the waters there did look deep and calm, too. But by the time I done think all a that, I just wasn't in the mood to ask him about the bathing suit.

So I realise that it didn't have nothing for it but to do the same thing in town as I did doing in country. And that was to leave Ganesh up to he enjoyments and find some a my own. That habit we did have of both a we being with each other in different ways continue to be – or maybe I should say seemed to be – the bond from which we could stretch in any direction we did want. But I probably wouldn't know how to put the idea in action if it didn't happen that my friend Mildred and she husband did also move up to Port of Spain, too – though they was living Belmont on the other side a the Grand Savannah.

It happen that Mildred did find out where I living and she come and look for me. Well, after that, for a while I really had a chance to enjoy being in town. Whenever she could spare some time – and that increase over these last years since we know one another – we used to go places together. Both she and Mr Thomas was trying to let other people do the work while them just managing the business, so I start to make sure that anything we get invited to, and Ganesh used to get invited to plenty things, I asking if Mr and Mrs Thomas could accompany we too.

When Mildred start to see how the ladies does dress up in the parties we was getting invited to, she say she have to take me in hand, one time sharp. I was really grateful for the dresses she did make for me to go to the parties in Ambard House, especially because it was in the district where the "Travelling Cinema Tycoon" – that is how they used to call him – did living. And why I mention him is because the people who went there used to dress up like if they just walk off the silver screen. You know the house I talking about? Anytime you went there, boy, somebody bound to remind you that it design after the Château de Vaux-le-Vicomte and tell you this was a baroque French chateau located in Maincy, France. And it didn't have a single time people say so that I didn't want to behave like I still in CM School and tell them they could go to France.

But plenty a the parties used to make me think that Ganesh fears about the city was coming true for me too. It was like nobody at any a the parties we used to go to did really want to have a conversation with either me or Mildred. Sometimes you hear the fellas talking more seriously among their self, but most a the people would just be saying words out loud that not stringing together to say anything that worth listening to. Still, it was interesting for a while to look at them and to see how the houses they was living in was so beautiful.

Mildred used to say that I does look like Rita Hayworth, so she start to dress me like Rita Hayworth – except that my hair was a little longer and not cut right, so she had to pin it in place to get the different lengths a curls that Rita hair used to be style in. For all the daytime things I used to wear my Doris Day dresses, and that wasn't so different from the bodice and skirt I used to wear my whole life, but the rest a the clothes she make for me wasn't like nothing I did ever wear before. I did really really like the long strapless dresses and shawls that Mildred make for me to wear in the evening. Not that any a that ever really help me to fit in, which was the aim a the whole project what come into my life so unexpected. Instead, them dresses probably cause plenty thing that show me that I don't belong, and make me sure that I don't want to belong at all.

In fact, when I remember one nasty incident in the early days, I does still feel like vomiting up to today. These two women walk up to we one time and one a them say, "We have been watching the two of you. You wear such beautiful clothes." Then the other one start feeling the cloth between she fingers like if I is a dead mannequin in a showcase window. "Where did you get this dress? It can't be in a backwater in south surely?" Mildred didn't say nothing and I didn't feel it was my place to say is she that make it when she right there and not saying nothing, so I just say, "Oh I really can't remember. I have it so long." So, I mighta be able to forget that part a the conversation, but when they walking away we could hear one of them say, "Life is so unfair. I wish I could look like that. They have such good skin and beautiful hair and did you see the body in that strapless dress? Did you see how the dress fits her as though somebody painted it on her skin?" The other one turn round and tell she, "Don't be an ass, darling! You cannot imagine the kind of life they were probably living before all this liberal nonsense bring them here amongst us. I would advise that you never let yourself compare yourself with them and you sure do not want to be anything like them. I remember the nasty smells and mud around the barracks when Geoffrey took me one day to watch them going at it. Darling, they spend all their free time either drinking rum or fucking like rabbits, or perhaps it's both. And they don't do it with any finesse. It's just hump hump hump. Geoffrey told me that there is another strange thing about them. It isn't the men who want to do it in more ways and more often. It's the women who demand it and if one man can't satisfy them, they have absolutely no problem just walking away from that one and finding another. They have pictures with their gods fucking like rabbits. Primitive, savage barbarians. I only spoke to them because I thought I would find out the name of the seamstress or the shop they're using. I have no intentions of becoming best friends anytime soon."

You could imagine how glad I was that Mildred was with me that day. She parrot them and say, "Don't be an ass, darling! Don't you worry your pretty head now, you hear. The bitch just jealous. You ain't see how she husband look like he is a good macomere macafouchette man. With she horse face, that is the only kinda man she could ever hope to get, a man nobody else don't want. Watch him good. You eh see how he is the kinda man who does only want to hang around with woman and talk woman talk. That is why she did have to go with somebody else to just watch what somebody else doing, because she certainly ain't getting none at home, and even if she want any outside, nobody ain't saying yes besides the woman hanging on she arm."

Mildred make me laugh, but that wasn't the only kinda incident that I did have to deal with from both man and woman. I was going for a walk around the savannah one day when I hearing, "Psst! Psst! The coolie baytee looking good enough to eat, boy." It wasn't the first or the last time that that kinda thing happen.

And then it had this time at a luncheon when this woman, who I used to notice watching me and Ganesh hard whenever she see we, come up to me. She say, "My name is Victoria Adams. My husband and I were introduced to you. Do you remember?" I didn't remember but she didn't wait for me to say so because she continue full speed. "I have been dying to meet you alone to ask for some advice. I am experimenting with the Kama Sutra, you see, and I was wondering which position you would recommend as the best." When I tell she I don't know what she talking about, she look at me like if I lying and walk off as if I do something to offend she. And that was the one and only time Miss Victoria ever talk to me.

And then it had all a them other times when I had to pull my hand away from one man or another who holding on to it too long, so I eager to agree with Mildred when she suggest that I should wear gloves. But it wasn't just in town this kinda thing happen. Don't let me begin to tell you about the times some big ugly man, smelling like the trench, try to corner me, and how much time I want to spit in their wife face when they come to take their man away, and they start watching me like if is my fault that it happen.

My name is not Ganesh and I never try to change how I talk or walk or think because a where I was. And that was and is and will always be the big difference between the two a we. I know that it didn't make things easier for Ganesh that that is how I is, but I couldn't help it, or change it, and I glad I never did. But when it get to be too much at these high-up people parties, I had to tell Ganesh to ask me to go with him only when I really must, and otherwise to leave me outta spending time with people like that.

I was always glad too, eh, that I did have Mildred in town with me because I realise that without she I mightn't have make it there at all. Indeed, she did know that it was becoming a little more than I coulda handle. So she take some action.

Mildred did remember good that I used to drive to reach by she when we was in Fuente Grove. One day she tell Ganesh, "Aye Mr Government Man. You know anything about the fact that your wife could drive better than your driver." When Ganesh laugh and say, "What you trying to tell me? That my driver can't drive?" She say, "No, I telling you your wife could drive and she could drive better than your driver." So then the whole story come out and Ganesh say if I want to get my license, he will make arrangements for Humphrey to take me to the Licensing Office and for driving lessons until I get my license and that I could use the car to drive myself if that is what I want. Well, Mildred did know people and both a we get we license in no time.

Once that happen, then we really start to go places. Mildred hear about the fashion shows they used to have at the Queen's Park Hotel. Well, you know the fashion thing was always serious business for she. But she carry me along so we could talk about the fashions without worrying about people hearing how we talking about the fashions on them, which is what did happen in the parties we went to. She say she have to teach me to see that, to put it in she own words, "Hats are the most important article of clothing for showing your social distinction."

And then she set about getting me some hats for all kinda different occasions. She buy some name Hattie Carnegie that was so expensive I never tell Ganesh how much they cost, even though he did get a set a different kind for heself too. I tell you, I did never believe the day woulda come when I woulda be wearing some a them weird things on my head, and I was well glad to leave them behind me in Port of Spain when I come back home. But at the time, as Mildred keep on repeating, "Girl, we having real fun and you know what, we deserve it, even if we have to mix with bitches now and again to do it." And I think to myself, well, if Ganesh could do thing to fit in, why not me too, if only for fun.

Mildred and me get up to a lot a mischief, I could tell you. We buy we first bathing suit together. We went to the beach together. We went cinema together and when Paul Robeson come to

Trinidad and Tobago and sing in Woodford Square, me and Mildred was there too, although up to that time I hardly ever go downtown except on one or two occasion with Humphrey to pick up Ganesh, just because I didn't have nothing to do when he was driving.

Up to now, I remember the outfit I wear for the concert. But that is probably because up to that time I mostly used to wear my Doris Day dress with the arm hole, square neckline, fitted bodice and wide skirts what Mildred first make for me when I was leaving Fuente Grove. But the time we was going to that show, Mildred say that things change up too much for me to continue to wear them, and she make a set a new clothes for both a we. Some people used to call them hobble skirt. I wear that with a off-the-shoulder blouse, a kinda shoes they call mules with funny shape high heels, a pearl necklace and earring set, and for the first time ever Mildred make me wear big round shades what Mildred call thick, sexy, multicoloured frames. That was probably the height of fashion late that year, because for the two Carnival before, the one that same year and the one before, I did wear a different style a dark glasses that Mildred self pick out.

I enjoy my first and last two Carnivals in 1947 and 1948. It never had mas in Fuente Grove and Four Ways; still don't have none here in fact. People who did like their mas used to head down Sando. So town was my first experience. The four a we had a good time, I could tell you, although it wasn't much different from going to the parties and watching people in costume. We watch them stand up in their lorries and open-back cars parading in fancy clothes, and they decorate their vehicles to match their clothes. It have plenty a them on float too. I did like the baby doll ones best. Every single one a them was wearing different different shade a pink and white from head to toe, from the little frilly lace umbrellas, baby bonnet and ribbon in their hair to the pink stockings and ballerina shoes on their foot.

We get a pretty invitation to a Bal Masque at the Trinidad Country Club in the shape and colours a the baby doll and all, and we had a really good time because the music was a little wilder than at the regular parties. The song I did like best that year was one that did come out the year before call 'Jump in the Line' by

Lord Kitchener. They did playing other songs by him, like 'Tie-tongue Mopsy' and 'Mount Olga' but I did first hear 'Jump in the Line' when the Roving Brigade did come down to the Travelling Cinema in Fuente Grove and me and the boy did happen to go that day for we film review for *The Dharam*. It didn't have no Carnival for about five years because a the war and that first one that I get to be in, the year after we come to town, was one everybody was glad about because they did expecting it, but then it had a lot a suspense about whether it go happen or not. Because of how the Governor was getting on, nobody was sure there was going to be one at all, because a all the striking and thing.

I remember, though, that that day in 1948 when we went to hear Paul Robeson was a kind a strange turning point for me. While we was in the square and the show was going on, I had a funny memory. I did remember how in the early days in Fuente Grove, Girdharie used to try to help me out by buying some a the coconut oil from me. When he was telling me how he could help, he say, "If you hear how Binti does say 'Get your coconut oil-cooooo-coooo-nut oil,' you will laugh." He was talking about how he used to take some a the coconut oil from me to carry for this lady name Binti Khan what he used to meet up with in the Chaguanas Market. He tell me that she does buy up all the oil she could lay she hands on, and the only limit is what she could get the cartman to agree to carry back up to Port of Spain, near Brunswick Square, where she living. But that wasn't the only thing I remember. I remember how I did feel sad for she when Girdharie did tell me that they make up a song in 1938 and call she name in it. Nobody on this island like to even imagine that something going to happen to them that going to make their name get call in one a them song. So I was remembering how exactly ten years before that day, Girdharie did tell me that people all about was singing about Madam Khan and he not seeing she in the Chaguanas market no more. So, I was thinking, look at me, I could be standing up right next to Binti right now and not know that is she. And I suddenly get a urge to find out more about she and to meet she that I couldn't keep down.

But I couldn't find out nothing about she that day. Everybody was singing along and having such a good time that you couldn't hear yourself thinking. So I went back afterwards to look for she, but a lady in the Square who remember she, say she did done dead a few years before. When I ask if she have any family, the lady say that them and all don't live there no more. But even though I didn't find she, that trip to look for Binti downtown was one that start to turn me a little bit from the good times I was enjoying with Mildred up to that time, and I will tell you about it after, because I think me and Ganesh did start to dislike town about that same time and for a few similar reasons.

While me and Mildred was having fun, Ganesh continue to try to fit in. One a the things I remember most is how I think he was looking for somebody to be like. Maybe that is why he start to spend time with the group a fellas who they did call the young Turks. When you go to party and thing, somebody was always saying the young Turks do this and say that. Is Kapildev who introduce Ganesh to them. Kapildev was one a the Turks he self. Sometimes they used to come by we house to eat and drink and talk. But Ganesh did start to talk about Governor Harris as the man he take for he model when they appoint him to be a Member of the Legislative Council in 1946, and them fellas like they didn't like that at all. They used to give him fatigue about how he is a good coconut, brown on the outside and white on the inside.

When Ganesh talk about how he impressed with the housing plans the Governor lay before the Council, Kapildev say, "Brother, let me tell you something. You new to this game, so you probably not seeing the whole picture. They talking about plans ever since the 1937 Commission that they sent from Britain to study the social problems in Trinidad and Tobago. Is almost ten years now since the Commission recommend the construction of new housing and sanitation facilities. But that is all they does ever do, talk big, present plans but never act, and in the meantime the people who the Commission find living in squalor still living in squalor.

"Trinidad's oil gives the government the ability to call big big figures for their annual revenue, but you would be sadly mistaken to think that our problems are not the same as the problems of other less resource-rich Caribbean colonies. They are the very same and we have to work together to work for the betterment of all peoples in all the colonies. These white people need to learn that they have to treat human life with more respect than they doing so far. I mean open your eyes nah man, and watch what go on right here for this elections. The British Empire Workers and Citizens Home Rule Party win six a the eighteen seats but they ain't get a single ministerial position. Why you think that is so?"

But Ganesh say, "I can't begin to understand how you could think that, far more to talk it? Look at what that Party do just because they ain't get none. Like allyuh did like it when Governor Clifford had to declare a state of emergency in January after they set the oil well on fire in Port Fortin. And like if that wasn't enough, they still storm the Red House at the end a the month. Is hooliganism you condoning? You can't really be saying that we shoulda tolerate that kind a behaviour.

When Kapildev leaving that evening he stop to tell me, "Girl, like your pati need some lessons so that he could understand how come he get nominated to the legislative council, just to pacify people who not taking too kindly to the fact that these people have been keeping us out of government for so long."

I was lying when I tell him, "Well Bhai, you know that I don't talk that kinda talk too much with Ganesh. So I feel *you* might have to help him to understand that for yourself. But I remember that my pati, as you say, used to report everything that Ranjit Kumar was saying when he was the president of the East Indian National Congress, and Ganesh did write in *The Dharam*, that he support Ranjit Kumar's call for internal self-government with communal representation, with half the seats in the legislature and one-third a the positions in the civil service reserved for Indians. He did agree that the end result a the government path would be unfair treatment for plenty Indians. Ganesh does always do everything very carefully, so maybe if you help him to understand, he will support your view too."

I not sure Kapildev did like the fact that I answer him back because he look at me and squint he eye and say, "But what is this? You as bad as your husband. You need to know that Kumar was copying Indian politics when he did that, asking for the same affirmative action that they were asking for the Harijans in India. Remember that they shut down Kumar one time already and make him drive taxi for a living. We should remember, too, that in India they deal with it differently because they were able to divert blame on the Indian elite for the Harijan problem."

I didn't answer him that time. I just smile respectfully because I didn't know how to explain that is not that Ganesh like Kumar as a person. He didn't know him as a person self until after we come to town and Ganesh start going to the Legislative Council meetings. It was just the position that Kumar was taking that did appeal to Ganesh. As a matter-a-fact, when Ganesh tell me Kumar is the one who bring Indian films to Trinidad and Tobago, I was thinking, "Oho, so he is the one who help Soomintra Didi and plenty other people to be the way they is." When I tell Ganesh so, he laugh, but only because he agree with me completely. So, when he did finally meet Kumar, he bring him home, but I didn't remember the name right away.

How it happen is that one day Ganesh call me up and say he bringing somebody for lunch and he want a normal rice and dal and something lunch. When he come, it was with this good-looking fella who look like he around my age. Ganesh introduce him to me as Prince Ranjit Kumar, so I ask if he was a calypsonian because only them does have Prince and Mighty and thing in front a their name. Both a them start to laugh, and Ganesh tell me no. He is a real prince.

I don't know what a real Indian prince was doing in Trinidad, though. I never get a chance to ask in all the years we did know him and he family, and I did forget about it until we talking about it now. All I remember is that a fella name Syed Hosein went to India to look for a imam to look after the needs a Muslims in the West Indies and somehow he get to talking to this fella and then he bring him back with him to Trinidad and Tobago. Kumar marrid and settle down right here down Couva side and then he get involved in politics and he was able to get Trinidad Indian to vote for him because he could talk Braj and Bhojpuri and, as I tell you before, plenty people couldn't talk or understand English too good, so he was like a godsend to them when voting time come.

After that speech Kapildev make in we house to me and Ganesh separately, I think there was a pulling away from the Turks. And then one evening, Ganesh say, "Look at this, Leela."

He was showing me something from a old *Port-of-Spain Gazette* from 8 March, 1898. Look, I still have it here in my folder. You see, it say:

> Trinidad has prospered wonderfully materially, but politically is a child at school. We are constantly told that we are not sufficiently educated in political matters to be entrusted with representative Government and it may be so. It is a question needless to discuss, but if it be true, at whose door lies the fault? If a parent not only neglects to send his child to school, but actively interferes to prevent him from acquiring knowledge, is the incapacity of that child when he becomes a man to be reproached to him or to the father? Questions such as these carry their own answer.

"Look at how long we saying this same kinda thing over and over, Leela," he say. "These fellas don't realise that you have to take responsibility for your own self and stop blaming other people for what they do or didn't do for you." Then he start to walk up and down saying, "Leela, these fellas puny, girl. They puny. Them just want to take over for taking over sake. None a them ain't no different from Narayan. With them is always what I could do even if I never do it before. Is never: let me sit down quietly and learn from those who know."

So Ganesh stop taking on the young Turks and other fellas like them, and one a the last things he talk with them was about Lord Harris. I remember good some a the things what he used to say. He declare in a loud voice: "Is exactly a hundred years since Lord Harris put forward progressive ideas that change Trinidad and Tobago for good, but like it going to take another hundred before a black or brown man will have enough power and respect from his peers to make any more progressive changes. Lord Harris was the man whose actions make it possible for me to go to a secondary school. Is through he that Queens Royal College was established, two years before my great grandfather arrive on these shores. Is he who also established the Model Training School for Teachers and the Public Library. He was the man who had the foresight to let we have these pipes with running water right inside of we house. So much of the road and railway we does still use is he doing. But like it ain't have room in this country for men like he or at least not for a black man who want to be like he.

After that Ganesh start to make friends with other members a the council. He try to work with them or at least find out about the kinda thing that they was doing. He tell me that even people who was there long time saying that how things pick up so much speed in the twentieth century that sometimes they can't believe what they seeing theirself. One man, who he become real good friends with, was a fella they did call Colonel Stanley. I feel Ganesh deliberately choose he because Stanley was in charge a things for the Imperial College a Tropical Agriculture and Ganesh was very interested in anything to do with education.

Because a that interest, Ganesh was involved with the establishment a the primary school-leaving certificate and the first exam for that was in 1948, same year Paul Robeson come and me and Mildred was singing and dancing in Woodford Square. I sure Ganesh remember he own schooldays and my experience and all too, and maybe even Soomintra Didi one who did want to get more schooling, and he make it he business to propose the school-leaving certificate as a way to select people to become teachers. Children with good passes used to get a bursary to go to secondary school and then from there straight to training college.

And I sure, too, he was remembering my days learning from Miss Mildred, so he promote the establishment of Handicraft Centres and Domestic Science Centres for all those who still didn't pass primary school exams. Then he supported the idea of free education what they bring before the legislative council in 1946, but, as you know, that didn't happen until 1961, after he did done leave the country long time.

When Ganesh start to work on thing to do with the Imperial College was the time that make him become the kinda person who was ready to leave. He tell me he see with he own eye a letter from the principal a the Imperial College telling the principal of a school like the one Baba carry him to that he should discourage non-white students from coming to college because the white students does make things rather unpleasant for them and this is not conducive to a good learning environment. Ganesh revive talks about the Imperial College that they did rest down since 1943, and he ain't stop until the discussions end with the college getting the 300 acres a the Bamboo Plantation in Valsayn what they have up to now.

When it finally get there, he come home and tell me with a smile, "You know what, Leela, it have another thing that happen with the ICTA now that I hope everybody seeing and appreciate what I really achieve there. They stop talking so damned much about the connections between ICTA and the Dominions and other parts of the Colonial Empire. And I say is high time because that is the way it should be."

By that time the 1950 elections was coming up, Ganesh say things so tense that when he get up in the morning he used to be happy to just stay home and siddown on the porch and read. He say he don't like to think that he have to go to Government House on them days when he didn't have no choice. The 1950 election had plenty more competition that the 1946 one. It had one hundred and forty-one candidates, and more than half was independents – ninety a them to be exact and all a them was contesting just eighteen seats. After the elections, Ganesh was complaining even more than he was before. He say that they calling the Legislative Council the Hindu council now, because so much a the fellas identifying their self as Hindu, and what worse is that they eh fraid to speak up and say so unlike the earlier batch a fellas who did have the good sense to try and fit in. He say that the talk and the mood he picking up making him frighten about what going to be waiting down the road for people like we.

That same year I remember when Beharry come to look for Ganesh. He come to ask if he could change the name a we Institution, what we used to call TTIIC for short, to the National Council of Indian Music and Drama – NCIMD. I didn't like that at all when he come and put the plan to Ganesh, because you couldn't even pronounce that name self. And I suppose I did also feel we losing something that we shoulda be holding on to, but Ganesh was happy. He say the work must go on and it good that Beharry and he sons and Swami and Friends carrying it on.

Beharry son, Suruj, did start going to the Imperial College, and Baldeo, the second boy, did nearly finish with Naparima College by that time, although the three girls what did come after them had a good few years to go still in Naparima Girls College. When Suruj did get accepted for the three-year ICTA programme, Bhowji did call to tell me, so I did done know already. She was so proud a he and talking so fast and so happy that I didn't have the heart to tell she that she have Ganesh to thank. But Beharry, like he understand better how it come about, and he was thankful. He tell Ganesh that Suruj and he friends continuing the work that Ganesh start and they form up a group at the ICTA too, and the older heads and the younger fellas does join up and make noise about everything and anything that they seeing happening what they don't like. I tell Ganesh I feel like that self is their motto, although maybe they ain't realise that: Make Some Noise.

But is thing like that what used to make me feel sometimes that Ganesh right when he talking about international perspective. When they making noise and you can't understand what they trying to say through all the noise, I used to remember Baba talking about how he watching developments in the government and he glad to see that Sir Samuel Wilson making speeches about the eighty-four acres estate they give for building the College. And now Suruj getting a chance to go to that same college. I thinking that all the excitement a the politics stopping them thinking about such things at all.

I thinking: Look at how Baba own son come and make that eighty-four acres grow into three hundred. That is how we should be helping the young to think instead a encouraging all the noise. But maybe nothing didn't change since Ganesh time and that is why the noise was important. When I tell Ganesh what I thinking he say, "Leela girl, I just have two things to say to that. One, via colendi haud facilis. Two, I don't know if Beharry have enough investment in land for it to be worthwhile that the boy doing what he doing. So maybe noise is all we could make right now, until we figure out exactly what we want and what are the best ways for we to achieve what we sure we want.

But that wasn't all that take place after the 1950 elections. All kinda things really start changing you hear. One a the things they start working on right away was how to give we a face internation-ally, and the steelband become the best sign for that. Up to now

I still have pictures a some a the young boys from when I did see them coming round the savannah for Carnival. They used to have their pan hanging around their neck just like how the tassa boys does hang their nagara. I remember how good I did find they looking and sounding, and I was thinking that that was a good face for people to associate with we.

So when they make the Trinidad All Steel Percussion Orchestra, TASPO they used to say, to stop the fighting between all the little steelbands at the same time as they was making them into the face a the country, I did think that was a boss move and Ganesh agree with me. They send them on tour to England and they represent we at the 1951 Festival of Britain. I did tease Ganesh too bad about the fact that the young Turks was the force behind that one and you have to give credit where credit is due.

But by that time I could see clearly that the kinda good thoughts and grand ideals that Ganesh had about government, and he opportunity to be in government, did start to shrivel little by little and he didn't laugh with the same joy when he did first start to observe what governing mean. I tell you I see it happening with my own two eyes and I kinda understand because that was how my own mood did shifting too. When I ask him what he does do whole day when Humphrey drive him downtown, he tell me that he does be reading. When I say, "Whole day???!!! That worse than when we was in Fuente Grove." He say, "Yes. Whole day." He say he working he way back as far as he could go, while he have the chance, through all the Hansard records of the debates and Governors' reports in the legislative council from the most recent sittings right back to the ones that escape the fire that cause the Red House to turn red after the water riots in 1907.

I did laugh at that because I didn't believe he really mean it. But he insist with a serious face that if he could accomplish that, he will have a sense a the background against which he live he life that will help him to make sense a what cause he life to be what it is. And more important, it will give him a chance to know where and how he could contribute to the development of we country. Ganesh say that sometimes he does walk from the Red House to the library and spend he hours there happily every day as usual, or sometimes he used to just sit down a little bit in Brunswick

Square and think about things that he done read. The name a the square did change to Woodford Square more than thirty years by that time, but people used to still say Brunswick.

But by the end a 1951, I would say, none at all of the excitement what he did start off with was there any more. Still, all the drama a the last few years did make the clock tick very fast while we was in the city, and although we didn't know it for sure yet, we did sense that it eh have long to go in this place again. And is so self it happen, because by the next year and a half we did gone from that place for good.

CHAPTER 10: AFTER THE MBE:
LIFE IN LONDON AND ELSEWHERE

Now most people does think that 1953 was we greatest year because a how that year Ganesh get the MBE, same time with Sister Florence Kernahan, the Principal of the Catholic Women's Training College, who get it for she work in education. But it had something else about 1953, boy. It was like we was done feeling what that man sing about ten years after – something was blowing in the wind. Perhaps it not important to the story, but if I remember correct, 1953 was the year that Rita Hayworth divorce Aly Khan and that was probably the only piece a good news I did get that year.

Up and down the place had trouble that year, although I have to admit that, as Ganesh tell me, maybe it did always have trouble. He say I was just not paying attention before. But there in town like you was always more conscious a the trouble and in them days I was feeling like how I was feeling when Baba dead. It could be because we did have to deal with death again and again in them couple a years, eh. But the point is that I was feeling just like when Baba dead, and I remain uneasy so in them years until I finally come back home and only, little by little, I start to feel normal again.

I remember how me and Ganesh siddown in the kitchen one morning and he going through the papers like he used to do every day. Then he jump up suddenly and say, "But what the arse is this I seeing here?" And then he read this piece a the newspapers out loud for me to hear:

The authorities with guns at the ready made a forced entry into the home of Dr Cheddi Jagan at 97 Laluni Street and also at his office at 199 Charlotte Street. Streets were cordoned during these raids at the break of dawn. The cruiser, *Superb*, and the frigates, *Bigbury Bay* and *Burghead Bay* are steaming towards British Guiana from Bermuda. Troops are being flown in from Jamaica. The aircraft carrier, *Implacable*, will bring further reinforcements from the United Kingdom towards the end of the week.

We did reading all kinda thing about communism in the papers – eh – for a good few years before that. One a the young Turks did even write up in the *Trinidad Guardian* how it had a red offensive growing in the West Indies. At first, I thought he was talking about the Red Army Steelband what was representing the country all over and did go to British Guiana in 1947 to do that. But after I done read the article, then I see that he was calling for people to rally around something he calling democratic anti-Communist sentiment and he was warning the population that they have to do that fast.

We was accustomed to that kinda talk from them by that time, because the young Turks used to give real pressure about all kinda thing, especially about the oil industry and how it running like a country with its own set a laws. They did have a newpaper, too. I can't remember the name of it no more but I remember reading something about how it inconsistent with they manhood and self-respect that the citizens a South Africa, Canada, Australia and other places like that – the ones who running things in the oil industry here nah – should be getting the same rights and privileges in this country which the citizens a this country wouldn't be able to get in them country. But Ganesh say that the fella who say that was always more radical than the rest a them and he not sure they have any consensus about anything, so is better not to treat anything they saying too serious.

I have that old thing what they did write about the red menace somewhere right here. You see what he say: "We shall be rudely awakened one fine day to find that the Red termites, whose headquarters are in Jamaica, have gnawed their way into all the West Indian territories. They have a well thought-out plan for infiltrating into all the West Indian territories and have found a convenient vehicle in the Caribbean Labour Congress." You see how he say that the red offensive was aiming to "destroy British rule in the West Indies and to establish a Communist West Indies in its stead and they already had their henchmen in every West Indian territory." That kinda Narayan talk you reading there was exactly why Ganesh didn't like the young Turks too much after a while, but still, although we was reading that kinda thing from them and other people for a while, none a we wasn't expecting what we was hearing about in BG in '53.

But things really begin to unravel towards the end a May 1953 when it start looking like the trouble in this place was more about race than political choice or class trouble or oppression of labour. And that is when Ganesh really start to worry. As usual I get the story in bits and pieces. First first Ganesh say, "If I tell you the latest, Leela, you wouldn't believe. They name a street after the Prince in St James and they make him a alderman on the Port of Spain City Council. Talk is that they do that just to keep him in line. I hear with my own ears that they using him and he Constitutional Reform Committee to delay things so that other parties that the Americans and the British Government support-ing could get the time they need to get ready to stand against Ayodha and them other fellas in the next election. It look to me like for some reason they fraid them fellas and I don't know why."

While I know it was Ranjit Kumar he talking about as the prince, it was hard to follow what Ganesh was saying because, just before that, it did have big celebration when what everybody was calling the unification a Hindus take place. That is what they give Ganesh the MBE for in 1953 – and make me a kinda widow just before I turn forty. I didn't get no warning self and didn't even know I did become one and so they take away my choice to commit sati – if I did want to exercise it. They say they give the MBE to Ganesh for he role in helping with the Incorporation of the Sanatan Dharma Maha Sabha outta the different organisations that was trying to talk for the same set a people at the same time.

I myself did think that was something to celebrate and I was glad they saying that Ganesh did have a role in it because a how I was feeling about my town experiences. I did have to stop most of them anyhow soon after the Paul Robeson concert because I had to cut down on going to lime with Mildred when Pa come and get sick.

When I went to see him one day and notice right away how he really couldn't do nothing for he self no more, I arrange for Sonachan to take over the shop and I bring him to live with we here in town. When we carry him by the doctor, he say is heart troubles, which is what most a we end up dying from anyway, and Pa have to watch what he eat and he have to make sure and walk everyday. Is so I get to know right around St Clair real good in them days because we used to try to walk at least as far as the Grand Savannah, and if we couldn't make it that far, we used to at least walk around a block or two right around where the house was.

Pa remain in good spirits and he was very happy to be in town and to see the kinda houses people living in up by there, which was so different from the kind we was accustomed to all we life. Because we was so close to Kapildev and he family, Pa also get a chance to put things in place for Jawaharlal, Sarojini, Motilal and Kamala to get the one one properties he did come to own all over Trinidad from people who owing him debt for rum. Without talking about it, the Four Ways shop did done settle in all a we mind as something that Sonachan would inherit. But although Pa was happy, like once he done settle up them few things, he must be feel he eh have nothing else to do and he didn't last too long after he done put all a that in place.

One morning, me and Ganesh siddown to have breakfast like we always do before Humphrey drop off Ganesh downtown, but we waiting for Pa to come because from the time he come to live with we, he like how we used to just siddown together and eat and talk before the day start so he used to come to eat with we too. But when he ain't coming, I went to check on him and when I open he door, I see he was still in he bed. I get frighten one time and I eh go no further. I went back in the kitchen and tell Ganesh and he went in the room. When he come back to the kitchen, he tell me that Pa gone.

Ganesh hug me up and say, "You have to give thanks for that, Leela. Obviously, Krishen Bhagwan messengers come their self and he gone with them quietly." The DMO come and examine him and prepare the death certificate and Pa come and get buried far from home, quite up in the Lapeyrouse Cemetery, so while I could still go, up to now, to talk to Baba in the spot where he body help to give life to the trees, I does have to treat Pa as if he cremate and imagine him in Vaikunth when I talking to him.

I did real glad that Phua come for Pa funeral and decide that she going to stay with we to keep we company. So she come and she spend the end a she days with we too. Sometimes Humphrey used to carry she visiting wherever she want to go, but she never leave we house to sleep a single night anywhere else after she come to be with we for Pa funeral. In the days after the funeral, it wasn't Ganesh but Phua who used to read *Ramayan* and *Gita* every evening for the few neighbours, like the Kapildevs, who didn't mind supporting we through this time by coming and taking part in that. Sonachan did play son part for Pa funeral and Ganesh quarrel with Soomintra Didi until she agree to let Jawaharlal and Motilal join him and them stay right through until the bhandara with we too.

But I did think that Ganesh woulda do the readings. As I tell Phua, "Is not as though he performing any ceremony, he woulda just be reading." But Phua say, "Better safe than sorry. A son-in-law can't do funeral rites for he father-in-law. It not allowed." When was she turn the next year though, Ganesh do everything for she, including the readings, all by he self. Phua funeral went to the banks a the Caroni river, because after Pa dead, Ganesh start adding he voice to everybody else one that was lobbying for the right to cremate we dead. Like Pa and Baba, Phua just leave she body there and walk away. When we find she in the morning, she did done put she self in the correct position and she had she two hand on the *Gita* on she chest. When is my time, I hope I will be able to leave this world and go away to the next one just so too.

But although we do all a this right kinda ritual thing for Phua and Pa, the difference between the two a them funeral in town and Baba one in country was more than I could bear. The whole village and all Baba family from all about did come to Baba one, and although you did feel sad because he gone, it had so much thing to do and so much family to help you to do it that it did make it worth doing. But it was so hard in town. I did feel like if it was just me and Ganesh alone because almost everybody else who coming did come like strangers. Nobody ever ask me if they could help me wash a cup self and if the Kapildevs didn't lend me two a their housekeepers, I don't know how I woulda manage the work for just the puja side a things.

Ganesh get a pandit I didn't know, but I was very grateful that at least he get one that have he own nau to do everything for him. I never thought I woulda feel so helpless to take care a something that in a different place I wouldn't a think twice about. I was so glad when Beharry and Bhowji, Swami and Partap and they family come up eh, I can't tell you. Because although Mildred and Thomas stay with we right through, it does help when somebody know that they have to help you to make sure about little things – you know like the gold to put in Pa coffin because he dead in Panchak.

But after everything done for Phua bhandara, it was like I start to collapse inside a myself and the emptiness a we life start feeling real bad for me. The only good thing was seeing how Ganesh didn't shame that he had to have a shave head, and he tell me heself that he take off he hat proudly in Government House. He laugh, though, when he say he could do that because he was sure it didn't have nobody who woulda come and pull he churki. Otherwise things did start feeling very dark and I start to walk far far from the house everyday, roaming like how I used to roam when I was a child.

And then one day, just so while I roaming, I remember about the Dr Vincent fella who name Stewart did call for Pa. And now that I start to think about it, I find how I also start to behave like a mad lady, asking any and everybody I seeing where I walking if they know a Dr Vincent. Grief is a helluva thing, you hear. You does do thing that ain't make no sense when you think about it. But anyhow you take it, crazy or no, I couldn't find this Dr Vincent at all. The closest was when somebody tell me that they remember a Dr Vincent Tothill who had a friend they used to call Lord Stewart, who went back to Scotland after spending years loafing somewhere in south. But the lady say both a them did living south side, not up in St Clair. When I ask if is Four Ways they was living, she say she never hear about that place. So then I ask if it was at the Coeur de Jardin Estate and the lady say that that sounding vaguely familiar, but sorry she not sure.

I start walking even further from the house after that and I used to console myself with the idea that I was discovering all the places where Binti Khan used to sell my coconut oil in Woodbrook and St James. But thinking about Binti make me want to go back to Woodford Square because when I did go back after the concert, I notice what I didn't notice that day. The place was full a homeless people, many a them Indian. Ganesh tell me afterwards that the Government clear them out for the concert, and after that they just let them come back out from the hospital and gaol where they did lock them up. That was just a quick fix so nobody wouldn't see how much a them it have with no place to be, and how much a them was in family groups – mother and father and children. Ganesh say that he used to be so sorry for them, but no matter who he ask, nobody didn't want to talk about them.

He ask the Governor and all and the only thing the man tell him is that they end up in a bad legal gap because, when they end the indenture system, they didn't put nothing in place for the final batch a people what come from India. When they five years up, a few a them agree to continue to work where they was indentured, but plenty a them come to town hoping they could get a ship to take them back home. Everyday they eating and sleeping in the square, hoping that the government will see them and do something for them and everybody playing they blind around them. Ganesh say he don't want me to go back to the square because he went through that already and he don't see why I should want to go through it too. He say that I wouldn't be able to talk to them self because I wouldn't understand them and they wouldn't understand me.

But even though Ganesh warn me, I feel like I have to go back and see them with my own eye again. I feel like I did forget what I did see that day after the concert when I went with Ganesh and Humphrey. But when I reach there, it was exactly like what I did see on the first day. Every bench and every corner in the square, and on the pavement underneath the eaves a the shops in and around Woodford Square, you seeing them looking like just a bag a skin over bones khukray on some bench with their elbow on their knee and their hands cupped and pushed forward to take anything anybody willing to drop in it.

One or two time, I try to talk to them after I put a shilling in their hand, but most a them refuse to look at me in my eye and the one or two who do watch back at me only say a word or two in a language I couldn't understand, which is exactly what Ganesh did warn me about and what I did done experience already. That is because before that I sometimes used to see one one up by the Savannah near to where we did living, and same thing they used to be doing. One or two time I did try to talk to them. One a them did try to answer but all he say was 'English na bol'. But is there in the square that what happen to them hit me in my heart like a hammer. It had plenty room for real committee work there, but up there is exactly where I didn't have no committee, and I didn't know what I alone coulda start to do because I couldn't ask them what they want or how they feeling and I didn't have no set a ladies with me who woulda help me to do something, like how I did have in Fuente Grove. I think, too, that Phua used to be the driving force for so much a that kinda thing I used to get myself involved in doing, that like I didn't know how to do it by myself now that she did gone.

And then the final crash come. Must be was just a day or two after I went to the square, Ganesh come home and he wasn't looking too good at all. I watching, but I ain't saying nothing because I know that sooner or later whatever eating him must come out. Finally, he say: "Leela, today I see something that wasn't meant for my eyes. It happen by mistake. Was a letter from the Governor to the Colonial Secretary. The Governor say that the suspicion that they did have that the East Indians in the colony was organising politically along racial lines had finally been confirmed. He say that one a the leaders gained his wealth by dubious means and he is the one to fear the most because he is leading the community towards East Indian political dominance in the colony through the inner core of pandits in his organisation.

"The Governor claim that he have reports that the pandits are this leader's agents in every Indian community and where this man does not have close connections with the pandits, his solicitor does. The Governor go so far as to accuse the Indian High Commissioner of being in league with them and that Her Majesty's government needs to beware of the Indians just as much now as the government has been doing since 1857, when another Queen occupied the throne."

And then like if to really crown things off, same time on the radio they was playing the calypso what Mighty Killer did sing the year before name "Indian People with Creole Name":

What's wrong with these Indian people
As if their intentions is for trouble
Long ago you'd see ah Indian by the road
With his capra waiting to tote people load
But I noticed there is no more Indian again
Since the women and them take away Creole name.
Long ago was Sumintra, Ramnaliwia, Bulbasia and Oosankalia
But now is Emily, Jean and Dinah
And Doris and Dorothy

Long ago you hadn't a chance
To see an Indian girl at a dance
But nowadays is big confusion
Big fighting in the road for their Yankee man
And see them in the market they eh making joke
Knocking down nigger people to buy they pork
And see them in the dances in Port of Spain
They wouldn't watch if you call by ah Indian name.

As for the men and them I must relate
Long time all they work was in cane estate
But now they own every theatre
Yes hotel, rumshop and hired car
Long time was Ramkaisingh, Boodoo, Poodoo, and Badoo
Now is David, Cooper, Johnston, Caesar, Cephas Alexander

And I start shivering, like when Pandit Dan did say "Saubhagyavati Bhav" when I bend to touch he foot after mine and Ganesh wedding. I was thinking that sometimes it does be amazing to realise how the music in this place does reflect exactly what some a the people thinking and feeling or fearing. But you could see from all a that that things was heating up in the place in ways that none a we did like, and it wasn't so outta the blue when Ganesh continue. He say, "Leela, this is a serious talk we must have today, girl. Things start off bad for me in Port of Spain the first time and I feel like things getting bad so again. They make me a member a the Order a the British Empire, but they treat me like if I don't know what is what. I fully aware a the whole history a that dotish award and I know exactly why King George V institute it in 1917. I know also that it come last in the order a the awards that the crown does give, and I want you to know that it eh really matter to me and I don't even know why they give it to me, but I like what I might be able to do with it. For instance, I don't mind being in England to see the coronation a the Queen. But it have some other things I want you to understand before we talk about that.

"You see I have been doing some thinking and I think that Bap was a very competitive man and he put me in a position I couldn't cope with very well. And right now I thinking that I do as much as I could to satisfy the longing my father had to see me become a man of substance and importance. I live the whole a my life for he, but I must be take after my mother because I don't have no ability to compete for nothing. I want to spend the rest a the little time left to me doing what *I* want, instead a for the sake a he. In this Crown Colony system, I was nominated as a member a the Legislative Council and therefore, as they say, entitled to serve during pleasure. Well, the pleasure done. It over.

"I have mixed with any and everybody in these circles and even among the best a them I find the same thing. Them fellas does just like to see they name in print next to something they say that will make people admire them. They worse than the people who Phua say like to skin their teeth for pictures in the papers about their charitable donation, when they don't even begin to know the meaning a charity. It ain't have nothing here to give meaning to my life and it too late for me to start over with that knowledge in mind. I going to take my friend Colonel Stanley up on he offer to visit him in London. He say I could stay as long as I want on he family estate. I think I will spend a year – take in the four seasons, see something of Europe maybe, who knows? And then I will come back home and we will decide what we going to do with the rest a we life. Will you come with me?"

I didn't answer because I was thinking to myself that Babu born in 1853 in India and come to Trinidad in 1867 and exactly one hundred years after he born, he grandson, who he hold in he arms and bless, want to leave here and go to England. And is the same kinda politics that causing the movement each time. Maybe that is where the journey did bound to end for Babu lineage because Kaka children and all gone there and we not in touch with any a them anymore. Fyzabad Phua didn't have no children. I did forget about the cousins that day, but I feel them gone too, because none a them don't live right here on the rest a the 100 acres block what I telling you the three sons did buy to settle down in Trinidad. All a dem sell and move because the oil companies was paying good money for the land, even when they didn't find oil.

So that is the end a that, I thinking. When Mandodari ask for the boon for she husband lineage to dominate the earth and all the descendants of the great lineages – the Raghuvanshis, the Chandravanshis, the Suryavanshis, the Yaduvanshis – down through the end of the first charan of Kaliyug, the gods didn't hesitate to give she what she ask for. I thinking that eventually we going to all come up with some schupid explanation like, 'I want to see the coronation a the Queen' to honour that boon Mandodari did receive. But for me that wasn't the time yet. So when I do answer Ganesh it was only to tell him that I understand what he saying. But, if he wouldn't mind, I don't want to go with him. Ganesh seldom say no to me for anything I ask, eh, and this wasn't no different. So we start to put things in place for he to go that side and for me to come back this side.

Ganesh coulda call me afterward, but he never do that and he never give me a number for he. Instead, a blue aerogram come about a month after I leave Ganesh in Piarco airport and I turn around and drive away to come home here to Four Ways, after he climb up the steps to go inside the plane and I couldn't wave from the waving gallery no more. In that letter, he say he was enjoying being in London very much, that he join the Society for the Study of Inebriety upon the recommendation of Colonel Stanley, and after just a few meetings he start to get along very well with everybody who trying to deal with plenty different kinda people with mental issues, but mostly with patients with drinking problems.

He say that the doctors who working on these patients want to influence policy through the recently established National Health Service, and that they want to make sure that treatment for the inebriates should not be just a alternative to imprisonment. He say he wish he could come back home and put some a the things he learning from the doctor side to work for the sake a all the people in Trinidad and Tobago who suffering from that problem. But he eh ready to do that yet. He say he happy to be teaching the doctors he techniques in the meantime. He tell me, though, that he having a hard time getting some a them to listen when he talking about the temporary residence we have in this body, and how we have to wait in readiness for the one that come after, and be aware of how the one that come before might be affecting the present one. But that is alright, he say. He just feel very lucky to get a chance to do in London what he used to do in Fuente Grove for the people a Trinidad.

He say another thing that making him like London is the order that it have everywhere, from the way people does wait their turn to get on the bus and nobody don't rush to take you over like how they does do in Trinidad, as if, if they don't do that, they ain't name man. He say he like how the discussions he does have with Colonel Stanley and he friends is always about how to improve things. He say he very pleased to see that, unlike in Trinidad, people does call it like they see it with no fear.

He say one a the fellas in the group, who everybody does just call Smith, say that he want to dedicate heself to change the fact that British political life does work through who knows whom, and people outside a these tight little networks don't have a voice in anything that the government doing. Smith say that civil servants are in charge of what happens in Britain and that has to change. Ganesh say that he enjoying being among people who working for change and willing to make a place in their life for him. He say he like how you don't have to feel shame if you have ideals and he glad it don't have nobody who attack him like how they used to in Port of Spain.

He write that he was earning a decent income from he work with the patients at the hospital and he does not plan to return any time soon, what with the group a friends and the new life that he developing. I didn't get no answer to the letter that I write back telling him what I was doing here in Four Ways, and that I hope he will come back to settle down here with me. And I never get another one from him again until ten years pass. And after that it was only silence again. In fact, I have been living my own life for my own self so much in the last twenty-five years that I did nearly forget about that other life until you come here and I get Ganesh letter same time that remind me about the rest.

Here, in this place I love, I make a pattern for my days that is a lot like Baba one in all the years I did know him, except mine don't include walking about in the village, just right here round he property. I rent out the few pieces that Baba did reserve for pasture for people who want to plant pumpkin and sweet potato, and I does meet a good few people and so I does know what going on in the village and I does read the papers to get to know what going on in the country and the world.

I have a few friends who does come here from time to time, and it does be good to talk about old times sometimes, especially with Miss Mildred who does always spend a few days when she come since Mr Thomas dead. Their children take over the business and it really expand plenty since government start giving financial and technical support for small local business enterprises, and, as you know, they promote the garment industry more than any other, eh. The children even open a few shops in Tobago and Grenada and all.

Sometimes Soomintra Didi does come to look for me, and she children does drop in from time to time, too, especially when they want to show their friends how people used to live long time. Once a month, the Ramsumair Institute of Cultural Peace does have a meeting here and everybody who coming to the meeting does stay for a few days. One a the young people does write about we discussions in the newspaper where she working. We does talk about tolerance and what we seeing in the papers and we surroundings that demonstrating intolerance instead, and we does do a good bit a what they does call charity work and we does report on that and talk about what is not charity but does pass for it. It keeping me fully occupied and allowing me to do some good, I think. And that is the story a my life.

Before I wrap it up, though, I suppose I should tell you a little bit about the last letters I get from Ganesh, the first one ten years after he leave and the other one what I get recently. So much things did happen after Ganesh leave – Independence and all the changes that have been part a it – so I write to tell him about all a that and that is when I get the first letter in reply. At first it did make me feel very hurt and I start wearing capri pants, flat shoes and fitted tops like the star in *Tower House*. But afterwards, I come to terms with it because that letter put my mind at ease about a lot of things I thought I woulda have to see about. When nothing didn't happen after that letter, I did start to get worried again and I was thinking that I go have to get up and act, but then this letter come the other day and I think everything will be alright.

Ganesh start off the first letter by telling me thanks for my letter, which arrived at his new address without difficulty, proving how efficient the British postal system is. Then he say he sorry that he never write in all them years, but he hope I will forgive him if he tell me that he did finally get a job in a new kinda institute in England, a place call Kingsley Hall, that was doing the same kinda work he used to try to do in Fuente Grove. And he want me to know that he come and get married to somebody there and that is why he never write me. He say he didn't want me to be hurt or to feel I have to make any changes to the life I was living as Leela Ramsumair. Ganesh heself work on changing the law to prevent that kinda thing from happening, but we did never do nothing to change the status a we own relationship. So Ganesh did free to do what he do, you know, because for all the big fuss it had over mine and he wedding compared to the beautiful little one I did do with Stewart, in the laws of this world it wasn't no more real than the one I did do with Stewart, and in the next world is only the one with me and Stewart that matter.

And like something come and happen for Ganesh, too. In the letter, Ganesh say that when he meet that girl, he find that the more he see she, the more he want to see she. For the first time in he life, he say, he start to feel how Baba did tell him a person does feel when he meet the one that belong to him. He say she name Patricia. He say they have a son and he name the child Leon in honour a me, because he say that although Patricia have blue eyes and I done know the colour a he own, the child come out with dark eyes and they full a mischief like mine, and from the time the child born and up to now, every time he look at the boy he does think about me. But Patricia don't know why he call the boy that and he want to keep it so. He finish the letter by saying that one day he will come with the boy and introduce him to he heritage in Trinidad and Tobago.

I never answer that letter and I never hear another word after that until last week when I get another letter reminding me about how he did tell me about Leon. In this last letter he write, he say the boy coming to Trinidad, and although he still calling him a boy, he is really a grown man now and Leon wants to bring his girlfriend with him here because he want to discover he black roots in the Caribbean. Ganesh write to find out if I would mind letting the two a them stay with me. I say yes they could stay, because while I was writing I didn't feel like I have a choice. But now I looking forward to meeting these two young people and finding out about Ganesh life in all these years that I don't know nothing about. I think that in that life he must be get the deeper sense a belonging that he did always want. This boy will inherit what is Ganesh own and I don't have to worry about putting things in place about inheritance after all, and that is also a relief.

The only thing left for me to do is to decide about dying. I thinking that maybe I should ask for my body to bury in Baba mausoleum, because I thinking that if I bury instead a burn, then I could remain anchored to the body and spend my days here forever after, just like Maria. I could see myself clearly, wandering among the trees and the flowers in this place that I love so much and which I always think about as loving me back as much in return. Unlike Maria, I will not roam because I lost. I will roam because that is what I want to do, that is what I have always done. But if burning and leaving this place behind is the only way to reach Stewart, then that is what I will decide to do. I hope Stewart will find a way to give me a sign about which is the right choice. I want to tell everybody so that when the time come, they will know what to do.

GHOSTWRITER'S DISCLAIMER

While I was growing up, I used to hear a great deal from my parents and other people from that generation about the great Caribbean statesman, G. Ramsay Muir, who went back to England just before independence. But later, Papa was the only one I had left and he could not remember things clearly anymore. When I asked him about the story of G. Ramsay Muir he became confused, though he remembered that G was granted the MBE in 1953. He was sure, you see, that he also remembered that the man had returned to his homeland in England, but that his Indian wife had not gone with him. She had returned to her hometown in Four Ways.

With that dribble of information and propelled by my fascination with the situation of doglas, the thousands of white-Indian romances and white-Indian rapes of every hue and shade across our island landscape – which was the story of how I myself came into being in the world – I tracked down the lady I thought of as Mrs Muir. Her story, as you will have read, is indeed vastly different from the one that people like my father seemed to vaguely remember. The white-Indian romance I uncovered was many other shades different than I had anticipated. I hope that in some literary heaven I will be rewarded for setting the record straight, to the extent that adding her version of things to other versions can accomplish that feat.

I have transcribed this story with very few modifications, exactly as Mrs. Muir, as she became known to a few like me, and as Mrs Ramsumair, as she was known to most others, or as Leela Ramsumair as she herself preferred and thought of herself, recounted it to me. As I wrote in the introduction, I did nothing with the tapes for a long time. I returned to them and sought their publication as a book because I think it provides some insight into actual historical events on the island, particularly between the 1930s and 1950s and even more into a woman's lot during that period as well as, to a degree, before and after.

I got Mrs Ramsumair to tell me her story because I told her that people knew about her husband but not so much about her, and that I would like to tell her story, if she would let me. In a way, therefore, this book is also about me tidying up loose ends, throwing out old things and trying to preserve properly anything that might be worthwhile for future generations. I hope the future appreciates it.

I was not able to fulfil one request that she had, and so I am forced to simply tag it here at the end. She said: "If you don't mind, in your book, I want you to tell people that my favourite filmi song was "Ai maray dil-e-nadan" and make sure you include all a the lyrics, you hear, because I think that is the only song I ever hear that I really learn the meaning for. I learn it because, although I didn't find the movie too interesting when me and my girlfriends went to see the movie *Tower House* the first time, I realise that that song singing the story a my own life, and I see its meaning. Or maybe it stick with me so much because that was the year we get independence and it was the same time Ganesh give me my own independence, too, although I didn't know it.

So here goes:

Ai mayray dil-e-nadan tu gam se na ghabarana (2)
Ek din to samajh laygi duniya tera aphsana
Ai mayray dil-e-nadan tu gam se na ghabarana (2)
Ek din to samajh laygi duniya tera aphsana
Arman bharay dil mein zakhmon ko jaga dayday (2)
Bhadkay hue sholon ko kuch aur hawa dayday
Banti hai to ban jaye yeh zindagi aphsana
Ai mayray dil-e-nadan tu gam se na ghabarana (2)
Ek din to samajh laygi duniya tera aphsana
Fariyad se kya hasil ronay se natija kya (2)
Bekar hai yeh batay in baton se hoga kya
Apna bhi ghadi bhar may ban jata hai baygana
Ai mayray dil-e-nadan tu gam se na ghabarana (2)

186

Ek din to samajh laygi duniya tera aphsana
Ai mayray dil-e-nadan tu gam se na ghabarana (2)
Ek din to samajh laygi duniya tera aphsana

Oh my innocent heart, do not be afraid of sorrow
One day this world will understand your side of the story
Make room for the wounds, not only for the aspirations
Oh my innocent heart, do not be afraid of sorrow

When something is already burning
What does it matter if someone adds a little fuel
So what if my life remains in this world only as a story

Oh my innocent heart, do not be afraid of sorrow
One day this world will understand your side of the story
Make room for the wounds, not only for the aspirations
Oh my innocent heart, do not be afraid of sorrow

What is the use of crying and complaining?
Crying and complaining are useless.
Nothing will change
A lover can become a stranger in a moment

Oh my innocent heart, do not be afraid of sorrow
One day this world will understand your side of the story
Make room for the wounds, not only for the aspirations
Oh my innocent heart, do not be afraid of sorrow

Oh my innocent heart, do not be afraid of sorrow
One day this world will understand your side of the story
Make room for the wounds, not only for the aspirations
Oh my innocent heart, do not be afraid of sorrow

Oh my innocent heart, do not be afraid of sorrow
Oh my innocent heart, do not be afraid of sorrow

I think she was right about that song being a good description of her and her life. And for that reason, in my mind she remains Miss Trinidad and Tobago, abandoned by the white man who wooed her so sweetly and by the black man with the blazing eyes who didn't know how to woo, and yet she keeps on keeping on still.

St Augustine
Trinidad and Tobago
30 May 2020

NOTE

The writer and publisher agreed that there should be no glossary included with the text of the book. The words that may be unfamiliar to non-Caribbean readers (and even some Trinidadian readers) are integral parts of the English/ Creole of Trinidad and Tobago. To have presented them in a glossary would have implied otherwise. However, since few readers will have a copy of Lise Winer's excellent *Dictionary of the English/Creole of Trinidad and Tobago* at hand (though it is still in print), we agreed that whilst all such words are readily interpretable from their context, we would place some notes on the Hindi- and Bhojpuri-derived vocabulary of the novel on the Peepal Tree website as a bonus for interested readers.

ABOUT THE AUTHOR

J. Vijay Maharaj has lectured at the University of the West Indies since August 2000 and specialises in cultural identity and cultural citizenship in Caribbean Studies. She was the editor of *Seepersad and Sons: Naipaulian Synergies* and *The First Naipaul World Epics: From* The Mystic Masseur *to* An Area of Darkness. She has essays published in a number of important collections including: *Fires of Hope: Fifty Years of Independence in Trinidad and Tobago*; *Beyond Calypso: Re-reading Samuel Selvon; Contemporary Caribbean Dynamics: Reconfiguring Caribbean Culture*; *Postscripts: Caribbean Perspectives on the British Canon from Shakespeare to Dickens*; *V.S. Naipaul's* A House for Mr Biswas: *Critical Perspectives*; *Critical Perspectives on Indo-Caribbean Women's Literature* and *Created in the West Indies: Caribbean Perspectives on V.S. Naipaul* as well as in journals such as *Anthurium: A Caribbean Studies Journal*, *Tout Moun: A Journal of Caribbean Cultural Studies*, *Journal of the Department of Behavioural Sciences*, and *The Journal of West Indian Literature*.